W9-BCL-931

A BIT OF A SCANDAL

Mary Rose Callaghan is the author of eight pevious novels, including *Billy, Come Home* (2007), *The Visitors' Book* (2001) and *Emigrant Dreams* (1996). As well as writing extensively for periodicals, she has published *Kitty O'Shea: A Life of Katharine Parnell.* She has been assistant editor of, and has written thirty articles for *The Dictionary of Irish Literature*, edited by Robert Hogan, and has broadcast stories on BBC radio. She lives in Bray, Co. Wicklow.

Also by Mary Rose Callaghan

Novels
Mothers
Confessions of a Prodigal Daughter
The Awkward Girl
Has Anyone Seen Heather?
Emigrant Dreams
The Last Summer
The Visitors' Book
Billy, Come Home

Biography
Kitty O'Shea: A Life of Katharine Parnell

A BIT OF A SCANDAL

MARY ROSE CALLAGHAN

To Lee

Best wishes,

Mary Rose Callaghan

BRANDON

First published in Britain and Ireland in 2009 by Brandon
an imprint of Mount Eagle Publications
Dingle, Co. Kerry, Ireland, and
Unit 3, Olympia Trading Estate, Coburg Road, London N22 6TZ, England

www.brandonbooks.com

Hardback ISBN 9780863223884
Paperback ISBN 9780863223969

2 4 6 8 10 9 7 5 3 1

Mount Eagle Publications receives support from
the Arts Council/An Chomhairle Ealaíon.

Cover design: Anú Design
Typesetting by Red Barn Publishing, Skeagh, Skibbereen
Printed in the UK

To Catherine, Celia, Ivy and Lia.
With love and thanks.

. . . and one night as I slept peacefully in an inner room in my lodgings, they bribed one of my servants to admit them and there took cruel vengeance on me of such an appalling barbarity as to shock the whole world; they cut off the parts of my body whereby I had committed the wrong of which they complained. (Peter Abelard, Autobiography)

It is a small thing I ask of you and one you could so easily grant . . . I beg you to restore your presence to me in the way you can—by writing me some word of comfort . . . (Héloïse, First Letter to Peter Abelard)

Prologue

At American dinner parties, my husband used to joke that I had been stolen from a Cistercian. People sometimes thought this was an obscure eastern European, rather than a Catholic priest. When the misunderstanding was cleared up and it was established that there was no such country as Cistercia, I would eye him to shut up. I never spoke about Peter, but times change, and Felicity is one of my oldest friends.

We met for lunch the Christmas after my husband's death. I was home for the first time in years and my son was coming for New Year, so I had time for visiting. The venue was an Edwardian redbrick in leafy Dublin 6, to which she had just moved. Everything had been redecorated, and on the grand tour I had said all the required things about the light, the white walls and the blond wooden floors.

From an upstairs bedroom, overlooking fields, Felicity pointed to a granite building with a cross on the roof. "That's a monastery through the trees."

I was familiar with the area. "I know."

It was in the middle of one of those tracts owned by religious orders all around Dublin, which are now being eaten up by housing.

As yet, nothing had changed there: the institution still looked dreary, the air of depression compounded by winter. For the past thirty years, that monastery had haunted my dreams. I had walked up its long avenue and down endless brown corridors which led nowhere. Was I in search of Peter? I don't know. Anyway, I had never found him.

She pulled up the window, letting air in. "Of course, you grew up around here."

I hesitated before going on. "I've been in that monastery."

"I didn't know you were religious."

"I'm not. A member of the order was a friend. . . . Remember Peter?"

"The Canadian? He used to visit you?"

Felicity and I had been flatmates in Sandymount.

There was a pause, then I blurted, "Did you know we were having an affair?"

"I knew something was going on! You spent so much time in your room. But I wasn't sure till later."

"My husband told you?"

She nodded, raising her eyebrows.

I laughed. "He had a habit of announcing it. It was a bit of a scandal."

Felicity looked intrigued. "Peter was at university, wasn't he?"

"Yes, doing a doctorate in theology."

"Wasn't that unusual for a monk?"

"I don't know, but he was at Maynooth. He used to go down on the bus."

She took this in. "I didn't know monks *could* . . . eh, have affairs."

"You're right—they're not meant to." I felt awkward that she had known all along. "Young people are foolish."

"It's not foolish to love."

Sometimes it is: the memory made me wince.

Felicity closed the window and we went downstairs. "He doted on you, but he used to put you down a lot."

"Did he?"

"Yes. He was dominating."

I didn't remember Felicity being that observant. I suppose I hadn't actually told her the truth because she had always been so, well, proper. Or perhaps it was because I had met her after meeting Peter. The affair wasn't something I was ashamed of, but neither was it something I shouted from the barricades. Maybe we need compartments in our lives? Or maybe it had been something to do with her being Church of Ireland? And having a legal fiancé and square middle-class parents who had lived on Ailesbury Road? How could they ever understand the story of Peter and me?

"You can't see all that land from the road," she said, halfway down the stairs.

"Hidden. Like life."

"What do you mean?"

I thought of my husband. "You don't know the future, then you stumble on something."

"Stumble?"

"Happiness. It was there all the time."

Felicity looked awkward. "It was terrible about your husband. We were all shocked."

It had been a short illness, which I couldn't bear to think about. "Life goes on" was one of my husband's sayings, "and it's just as well." His voice would now be for ever in my head. He used to say that work saved us all. I had my teaching job. A university is an Alma Mater, and I could lose myself in its concerns. Classes and committees kept me busy.

"I always thought yours was a marriage made in heaven."

"It was."

"You're managing all right?"

I nodded. "I have work. And my son."

"I've read your articles in *Art in America*. You're famous."

I laughed, shaking my head. I had achieved a few small things: tenure and a well-received book on Renoir. Some critics don't consider him a great artist, but I have a tenderness for his blowsy young women. Although often of questionable reputation, they were always portrayed with dignity and no moral judgement. He captures the joy and hope of life like no other painter.

"You were a coper, Louise."

"*What?*"

The difference between your idea of yourself and what other people see is sometimes amazing. "I was a mess."

"You were so glamorous."

"I didn't see myself like that."

I wanted her to stop, but she went on: "A beautiful young woman. I used to envy you sitting at the table, clattering away on the typewriter, lost under all that hair."

"You were the successful one—working for a bank and all."

"No . . . you were so self-sufficient."

She was wrong, but I couldn't say what I was thinking—how I might have missed my life. The thought of my husband caught my breath again. Memories of thirty years ago played like a DVD in my mind: of the night I had bumped into him, of the crazy months before. The chilly spring afternoon I had walked up the avenue to the massive hall door of the nearby seminary for an interview with Peter's superior.

Felicity chatted on. "The monks have sold the land—no vocations. We'll be overlooked by the new building. It'll be a southside Ballymun."

"A pity to lose the view," I said, but I wasn't sorry that ordinary people would live there: families with children. "Institutional life will be a thing of the past."

"Will Catholics have a married clergy?"

"It doesn't look like it. The new pope seems more conservative than the last—and that's a feat. But they'll live in smaller places, ordinary houses maybe. Some of them already do."

"Franciscans are one of the oldest orders."

"These are Bernardites."

"I thought they were founded by St Francis."

"No. At some time they split from the Cistercians. These are a more liberal branch mainly in Canada. They wear shoes, talk to each other, come out of the monastery, run schools and that."

I had known Felicity since the mid-seventies. It was odd to think of that being the last century now. Dublin had changed so much: faceless concrete buildings were everywhere and cranes criss-crossed the sky. The traffic alarmed me, and the new immigrants made the place reminiscent of New York, where I'd spent more than half my life. The Troubles were over, but the rest of the world had turned into an Ulster. We talked about old times and, of course, kids. Hers were teenagers and twenty-something, and in college, while Owen was thirty and living in an apartment. He worked as an editor for a prominent New York publisher and was missing Christmas in Ireland because he had to donate bone marrow to his half-brother, who had been diagnosed with leukaemia. My son was like his father—good.

Over lunch we agreed that Dublin had turned into a province of China, or Poland: you often met shop assistants who couldn't speak English. Bewley's had gone upmarket, and there were motorway tolls. Our faraway land of grilled grapefruit and poor plonky dinner parties was gone for ever. Today's young drank good wine and lived in purpose-built apartments. They flashed credit cards and were self-assured in a way we had never been. No one could have predicted that Ireland would be one of Europe's richest countries. In grade school in the States, my son used to beg for stories about my childhood: the freezing houses, unemployment, all the old bangers, the lack of money, the vandalised phone boxes. To him it was a Dickens novel: *Olivia Twist*.

"There've been scandals in the Catholic Church here," Felicity said, frowning.

"In America too. Our affair wasn't anything like that."

"How come?"

"It was consensual."

She looked doubtful.

"I was a grown-up!"

Felicity kept talking about the past, asking me if I had kept in touch with Peter. I told her I hadn't. A few years earlier someone had told me he was back in Canada, and still a priest. His voice now sounded in my ear: *"No one else will ever have me, I promise."*

"Why don't we Google him?" Felicity said.

I hesitated. "Well . . . he *was* planning to publish."

"Let's do it."

"I've never seen his name anywhere, but then, I haven't been looking up theology books."

Felicity kept pressing, so we went into the study and switched on the computer, finding about five sites for Peter. He was prior of a monastery in Alberta, which sounded like the one he had entered all those years before. There was an email address and a telephone number.

That night I wrote to him.

To: *Peterfan@bernardite.org*
From: *Louise@barnard.edu*

Subject: Happy Christmas
Date: 20 December

Dear Peter,

Isn't the Internet marvellous? I typed in your name and up popped this email address. I wanted to tell you my husband died last January in New York after a short illness. It was a difficult time for me, at first, but I'm better now. Did you know we had a son in 1977, Owen? He inherited his father's literary ability and has landed a job in one of the big New York publishers. I've been so lucky in my son, and can never help bragging about him. My life has been happy. How has yours been? I have often thought about you.

Happy Christmas and love, Louise.

I waited for a reply.

I felt sure there'd be one.

One

THOSE WERE THE days of long lunches.

I met Peter in an Italian café at the back gate of Trinity—Bernardo's by some strange coincidence. It's gone now, but I was Tim Farrell's lunch guest that day. He was editor of *The Catholic Trumpet*, a religious weekly, gone too—I won't say alas, although it wasn't a bad little paper if you were of that ilk. Tim was your typical journalist—fifty-something, with a beer belly, red face and thinning hair. The species was plentiful in Dublin then and frequented the city-centre pubs, consuming endless pints.

Tim always had a "real" drink to start, followed by a bottle of wine with the meal, then a couple of liqueurs to get through the afternoon. I couldn't afford alcohol unless someone was paying. That day he was downing a gin to warm up and offered me one.

"I'll stick to wine," I said—water was unheard of.

The weather was as usual: rainy and cold. It must have been early January, that hangover time after New Year. My poverty had made me value-conscious, so I ordered minestrone soup, followed by spaghetti Bolognese—the most filling things on the menu. As the waiter left our table, the door opened and two men came in. They looked ordinary enough in anoraks and jeans. The man who turned out to be Peter was about thirty, olive-skinned with black hair. He was wearing a baby blue sweater over a burly body: the first impression was tall, dark and too handsome. The other man was smaller: an American academic with wild grey hair, on sabbatical from a New York university. I recognised him at once, because of his hair, which had always reminded me of Einstein's. It was Dan Delaney. I had been in his politics tutorial when he had been teaching in college a few years before. Tim knew him too. Being an editor, he had an information file on everyone in Dublin. It was his business, he told me.

They stopped at our table.

Tim introduced me. "This is Louise, our regular reviewer."

I wasn't that regular, but glad of the title. It sounded important.

"Hi, Louise." Peter's smile was a toothpaste ad. At first I thought he was another American, but his accent was Canadian. His blue eyes were amused. "You're a journalist?"

I said I was freelance.

The professor didn't remember me. I was relieved, because my academic career had been inglorious. I had missed his classes and probably still owed him several essays. By some amazing chance we had had him as a tutor. It was unusual for Third Arts general to have someone distinguished, and even then I knew he was an important scholar. He had written several books about modern Irish politics.

More small talk was exchanged—I don't remember what, maybe something to do with the Troubles because the professor was researching a new book about them. Everyone was worried about the North: three members of the Miami Showband had been killed in an ambush when a UVF bomb had exploded the previous summer; and the Ferenka factory owner, Dr Tiede Herrema, had been kidnapped by the IRA in October. It had been a huge story.

The men crossed to their table and Tim poured my wine. It was white—the best Italian, he said. He was taking me out on expenses, so could afford to be generous. He was good to me, but I wanted a full-time job. Since no one ever paid freelancers, it was a battle to get a cheque. So when a "real" job was advertised in the back of the paper, I had applied.

STAFF JOURNALIST WANTED

Candidates should have demonstrated strong reporting and writing skills while working in the print media in Ireland or elsewhere. We are looking for a professional with a lively and engaging prose style, an eye for detail and an ability to work independently.

I was hopeful, because of Tim. He had tried to help me in the past, selling me an old office typewriter for £10.

In those days it was a case of "push and pull". You had to *know* someone. It's different now, like drinking at lunch. Anyway, I had been short-listed and interviewed along with two males—another freelancer about my age and a younger, slick-looking ex-seminarian. But I had heard nothing more. Then Tim phoned, inviting me to Bernardo's—surely a good sign?

In the middle of the soup, he looked up.

"Louise, love." His voice was gloomy.

I put down my spoon.

"Yes?"

He shook his head. "I'm afraid we filled that position."

My breath went. "With a man?"

He slurped his soup. "Sorry, love."

There was hypocrisy in his tone. So lunch was to break bad news—an appeasement.

"The ex-seminarian?" I said.

Tim nodded. "He impressed the board."

I finished my soup. The ex-seminarian had been a suck-up. Why couldn't he have stayed where he was? He'd no right to *my* job. But that was modern life: priests were jumping ship, as Vatican II hadn't lived up to expectations. After all the promises, nothing had changed. Holy Catholic Ireland was still in the Dark Ages: married clergy, contraception, and abortion were *verboten* and always would be. Despite Jesus being the son of an unmarried mother, there had been Magdalene laundries until recently, and if you got into trouble, your family gave you a suitcase. My own mother wouldn't have done this, but she was untypical. I was a lucky one in the Ireland of the day.

"They were impressed with you, too," Tim lied. "But . . . ah . . . he's done a bit of writing."

"Where?" I hadn't seen his by-line anywhere.

"He edited a magazine."

"Which magazine?"

Tim cleared his throat. "A mission magazine."

I had contributed to one in school. To my young mind, it had been a pathetic rag, with articles on St Martin de Porres and the masochistic saint who had cured all the lepers: Damian of Somewhere. So lunch was my consolation prize. A sop to Cerebus, except I wasn't a dog; I was an unemployed hack with rent to pay and delusions of grandeur.

I had put "journalist" on my passport, but had just been fired from a trade magazine, a boring monthly, where I was effectively the assistant editor. Was it my fault that I knew nothing about business? Or that the editor, when he bothered to show, was like someone from the French Revolution? He screamed and ranted, making work a nightmare. Everyone got the chop. My turn had to come.

Now starvation loomed. Pasta was the worst thing for my weight, but it was a slow-burning food and would last until the next day's breakfast. I knew about such things from my flatmate Brigid, who was hypoglycaemic.

The waiter plonked heaped plates in front of us.

"You promised to put in a word." I rolled the spaghetti around my fork.

Tim raised shaggy eyebrows, glancing sideways at my chest. "I know, love. I tried."

I ate furiously. I didn't know what to believe. Tim was obviously lying. He was like Charles Laughton in an old movie. As he concentrated on shovelling in the cannelloni, a blob of cheese fell on the napkin that was tucked into his collar. He wore the baby's bib in public as well as private, which was embarrassing. I knew because I'd been to his house: his wife, Phoebe, had befriended me.

He spoke with his mouth full too. "They're not taking on any more women."

They were the owners of the paper, the boys offstage you never saw. What did he mean by *more* women. There weren't *any* in editorial, as far as I could see. The only females were in the front office—drab secretaries, bookkeepers or receptionists. They always whispered cattily as I passed through on my way to the editorial room. They hated me. Tim had said this was my imagination, but it wasn't.

"You can still freelance, love." I wanted to scream: *stop* calling me "love".

"I'll pass on any book I can. In fact I—I have one here."

He took it from his battered briefcase.

I read the title: *A Guide to Modern Theologians.* It looked heavy. "How many words?" I said.

Tim was busy eating.

"Five hundred," he said through the cannelloni.

I put it in my shoulder bag. "Thanks."

It would be a few quid. The rent had gone up because Nigel, my ex-boyfriend, had left the flat. And Brigid, my other flatmate, was planning to desert to Kerry as soon as she could organise things. She had met a bearded farmer and was going back to the land.

Tim sighed. "You're good, Louise. At least you *will* be."

The future tense was deflating.

"But you're a woman."

"I can't help that."

"Did *I* say you could?"

I shook my head.

So much for women's lib. There had been a fuss about the *The Irish Times*'s women journalists (Maeve Binchy and co.) being paid less than the men, so they had demanded their rights. If I couldn't even get a job, there was no hope of *any* pay.

Then I got up courage—it was the alcohol. "If I'm so good, why do you change my copy?"

Tim coughed. He always slanted my articles to his way of thinking, which was pre-Noah's Ark on some things and liberal on others. You never knew which.

"It's my job," he said grumpily. "I'm the editor."

I was in the NUJ and knew this wasn't the case.

"More wine?"

He emptied the bottle into my glass.

The waiter brought another to our table. White wine was a lethal hangover, but I downed it like lemonade.

Throughout the meal, the two men stared across the room. Being the only customers in the restaurant, we were all conscious of each other. They smiled and I nodded back, as Tim kept topping me up. I had lost count of my drinks, so I covered my glass.

"I—I've probably had enough."

"Ah, drink up."

Tim thought the more drink he gave you, the better host he was. Before the meal ended, he had ordered another bottle and I kept pace. In the end my head was spinning. I didn't feel myself getting drunk, otherwise I'd have stopped—at least that's what I told myself later.

Tim went on talking. As things got fuzzier, I tried to focus on my own troubles. If I couldn't find someone for the flat, I'd have to move back home to my mother. Already we were having trouble replacing Nigel. Everything happened in threes: Brigid planning to move on; no job; and Nigel ditching me. He was a nerdy type, a French lecturer in Trinity. I had thought we were in love. Thinking of him, I swallowed back tears. I couldn't cry in public. People would think I was drunk.

At some stage the professor invited us for a liqueur, so we joined their table. It felt like the mail boat as the floor rose to meet me, except I was the only passenger.

To my relief, the professor didn't mention my missed classes. Peter pulled out a chair—I remember that detail exactly.

"You OK?" He steadied me as I sat down.

I nodded, afraid my voice was slurred.

It turned out Peter was doing a PhD—in theology of all things. The talk got on to the other man's book on the IRA, as the waiter took our orders. I had a Baileys Irish Cream, another lethal hangover. But it tasted like baby food, and I'd always had a liking for anything milky—because I was never breastfed, according to my mother. Condensed milk will do too. Or Complan, that grey-glue invalid food which everyone detested. Nigel had introduced me to Baileys on holiday, so it had happy associations. I downed one and then another, remembering zipping round Kerry in his Mini. Why hadn't things worked out between us? He had said I was uptight because I wanted to get engaged. I didn't look it, but I was the white-wedding type. Now my heart was broken and would take years to mend.

Peter was staring.

"You OK, Louise?"

The floor rose again. That dizzy feeling was the last thing I remembered clearly. Next I was throwing up into a urinal in the men's loo of the Lincoln Inn, the pub next door. How the hell had we got there? I didn't remember leaving the restaurant. Between my legs were four men's shoes. The strong smell was like the lions' cage in the zoo. But being male, my companions couldn't have brought me into the Ladies.

Next I was being helped into my Afghan coat. Then I was in the back of a taxi with Peter. Tim had fled, like a true friend. I don't know what happened to the professor.

"Take us to Sandymount," Peter said.

"It'll be ten quid if she pukes in my car," the driver yelled.

"It's OK. She's been sick."

Peter sounded an expert on drunkenness. His looks put me off from the start—I've always been suspicious of good-looking people—but my head was against his shoulder, as we took off in a southerly direction. Georgian houses flashed past and then the red-bricked, tree-lined boulevards of south Dublin.

"That coat smells funny," he said.

I pulled away. "Personal r-r-remarks are rude."

Soon we were turning into Serpentine Avenue, our conversation batting back and forth like a game of ping pong.

"Where do you live?"

"I'm not telling you!"

"Stop this nonsense!"

His voice came through a cloud. I was passing out again.

Home was a damp basement at the end of the avenue, but I couldn't appear there as I was; I knew that. The landlady, Miss Pym, might be back. She was something high up in the Natural History

Museum and, therefore, used to curious sights, but a footless tenant would be curtains. Curtains were one of her obsessions. She pestered us to draw them evenly—ten inches on each side. It was crazy because they were a foot short. Brigid had shrunk them in the launderette, and they would never look right. We circled Sandymount Green with Peter pestering me to tell him where I lived. I kept saying I couldn't remember.

"Oh, come now."

"Leave me alone."

Then he tried the soft approach. "Be a good girl."

"No. You're a creep."

"Why do you say that?"

"All religious are creeps. Fucking creeps."

"Watch your language."

"You w-watch yours!"

I must've told him in the end, or he got the information from my handbag, along with my key, because the next thing was we were trying my landlady's lock. Her home was a Georgian cottage with stone steps to the first floor. The upstairs was posh, compared to our dungeon. Landladies didn't worry about maintenance in those days—the word was unheard of.

The key didn't work.

Peter rang the bell.

Luckily no one was home.

He must have twigged that I lived in the basement, because next we were staggering back down the steps, me supported by him. Somehow we got down the path to the flat door under the front steps.

"You're heavy."

"You *are* a c-c-creep."

This time the key worked and he steered me down the dark hall to my bedroom. Then he was taking off my coat, removing my boots and putting me to bed. When I was lying down, he took off my skirt and opened my blouse.

"What are you d-doing?"

"Just lift your ass for a moment."

"My ass? That's rude. You're undressing me?"

"You'll be more comfortable."

I lay there in my slip, as he tucked me in.

"I'm leaving water beside the bed." His voice came from a long way away.

"Th-thanks . . ."

"Drink as much as you can."

"D-drink?"

"Water."

"OK."

I smiled in my sleep. I was safe in bed and someone had kissed me goodnight. I didn't know it then, but it was to have consequences in my life.

Two

I AWOKE WITH a terrible thirst.

My watch said nine o'clock. From the darkness, I decided it had to be that night and not the next morning. The top of my head was cut off. Where the hell had I been? What had I been drinking? White wine—Tim's expensive Italian. Oh God, my prediction about that had been right—I could hardly see. But I couldn't blame Tim. He hadn't poured it down my throat. I had been a willing participant in my own downfall. And the thought of Baileys made me retch. Where was the aspirin?

I crawled out of bed and groped in a drawer.

No luck.

I smelt of sick.

Everyone should get drunk once. That way you can't be so holy when others succumb. But it's so awful, once is enough for any lifetime. Slowly the afternoon came back: the restaurant, the Lincoln Inn, the bolshie taxi ride. I remembered shouting. What the hell had I said? I blotted that out. *Who* had brought me home? Then I remembered—the too-handsome theologian. I had made a holy show of myself, yet he had kissed me.

I went into the bathroom and ran the shower. Cool, clean water would wash away my hangover.

"Louise?"

Brigid was knocking on the door.

"Yeah?"

"You all right?" she called over the trickling water.

"Sure."

The shower never flowed properly, owing to poor water pressure, which was a problem all over Dublin 4. Nothing in that flat worked, and mushrooms grew out of the wall behind the pay phone. We were undemanding young people and never complained. Our flat seemed marvellous, because we had nothing to compare it with. Living away from home was bliss, although I did get on with my mother. We had a unique relationship and were more like sisters.

"I'll be out in a sec." I kept my voice light.

Brigid hovered, then the sitting room door banged.

Did she guess what had happened? She was a puritan and big into fruit juice and raw carrots. She hardly drank.

I dowsed myself in talc, then eau de Cologne. In my dressing gown, I tiptoed past her through the stuffy sitting room to the kitchenette. It was under the front steps in what had been the coalhole. The Super Ser gas heater was hissing and had, as usual, steamed up the windows. A cup of tea would cure me. Tea was my panacea for all things: the wonder brew I drank first thing in the morning, last thing at night and all hours in between.

Shakily I put on the kettle and ran a glass of water. "Do we have any aspirin?"

Brigid frowned. A national schoolteacher, she was marking a pile of copy books at the dining room table—not that we had a dining room, we just called the table that. She was the opposite of me—small and dark, while I was tall and red-haired. "You shouldn't take pills," she said.

Even a harmless aspirin was a chemical: you were liable to hallucinate. That was Brigid.

She was cross now. "You got home OK then?"

I nodded, puzzled. How could she know about my fall from grace?

"Phoebe Farrell phoned."

"Oh . . ."

"Tim was worried."

There was an awkward silence. *What* had Phoebe said?

Brigid stared. "You look terrible."

"I do?"

"Yes."

"I passed out in the Lincoln Inn. I can't remember much. It was after my lunch with Tim."

"He didn't see you home?"

I shook my head.

"Typical."

Brigid went back to her copy books. She had no time for journalists and didn't understand my obsession with becoming one.

"Someone got me into a taxi. A theologian from Maynooth. Peter something."

It was coming back in horrible detail: the pungency of the men's loo, calling Peter a creep, the taxi cruising up and down Serpentine Avenue, me refusing to say where I lived. He must have thought I was an alcoholic. But one swallow didn't make a summer. Thank God, I wouldn't be likely to run into him again, because I didn't move in religious circles. I should thank him, but there was the embarrassment of phoning. I would donate to the missions in lieu: thanksgiving for a safe homecoming.

No aspirin in the cutlery drawer, or the cupboard where we kept the tea tin.

"I didn't get that job, by the way," I said.

"Something will turn up."

Brigid was prone to statements like that: everything happened for a reason. What was for you wouldn't pass you by. We were all watched over by a sort of divine clockmaker. I didn't believe it, but she was the sensible half of our relationship and, despite being a bit abrupt sometimes, the most consoling friend in the world. How would I manage without her?

I sighed. "I don't think so."

"If one door shuts, another opens."

"Yeah, the emigrant ship." In those days people left Ireland in droves for London and New York.

"Stop talking like that." Brigid always treated me like one of her senior infants.

"Do you want tea?"

"No, thanks."

I sat on the couch in front of the heater, sipping mine. "I'm twenty-five, not five."

She kept on marking mechanically. "Who got the job, anyway?"

"The ex-cleric."

"The overweight guy?"

"Yeah. My head's throbbing."

"Drink plenty of water."

"I'd kill for an aspirin."

"I told you, you shouldn't take pills."

In the end I found an ancient Lem-Sip behind the tea tin and took it back to bed with two mugs of tea.

For the next few days, I had the Lady Macbeth syndrome. I kept washing myself, over and over again. No damn spots, but I reeked of something. It couldn't be sick; maybe it was unhappiness. Everything was awful. In a couple of months, Brigid would be gone, and that prospect was bleak. And money would be even lower: I couldn't keep on the flat by myself. I didn't want to go home to Ranelagh. It was only up the road, but a great distance in symbolic terms. I had left home and was a grown-up. The immediate problem was to find someone for Nigel's room. I had tried advertising in the evening paper, but there had been no replies.

"Maybe we should try putting a notice in Trinity?" Brigid said.

I was eating her fried cabbage. "I'll do it tomorrow."

"Then you can get a third person when I go."

That was something I didn't want to think about. The flat was sixteen pounds a week, so we decided on eight for the new tenant: that way it would be four for each of us and eight for me when she left.

I pinned a note under the arches at Trinity:

THIRD PERSON WANTED

To share nice flat off Sandymount Green. All mod cons.
£8 per week, plus bills. Garden view. Phone 695662

I added: Smokers Welcome.

We had hoped for a girl, but Declan turned up, reeking of a joint—the wording must have attracted him. He was right out of the Bolshevik Revolution: a ratty student of Russian, who talked about the rights of the working man, but stayed in bed all day. Trotsky was his hero, although he looked more like Lenin. He had the same foxy face, but his hair was long. He wore a huge navy guard's coat. Everything else was black: polo-necked sweater, jeans and sunglasses—even at night.

He shook his head when I offered my hand.

"Don't press the flesh, man." His accent was northern—later I learnt he came from Donegal.

"Oh . . ."

"Too bourgeois."

Brigid eyed him suspiciously. "I'm Brigid."

"It's Dec, man."

"And I'm Louise."

"Hi, man."

"Hi."

"Are youse long livin' here?"

"Since last September," I said.

"Cool, man," was all he said, looking round. "Cool."

He loved the flat. Our shabbiness appealed to him.

Brigid, a better judge of character than I was, hesitated about taking him in. She told him we'd have to check his references.

Then he took out a wad of notes like a gangster.

"How much are youse lookin' for?"

Brigid caught my eye.

I mouthed, "yes": I had never seen so much money.

She blinked as he peeled off the deposit, plus one month's rent in advance. He arranged to move in that day and went to collect his things.

After he'd left, I gloated over the money. It would take care of next month, and by then I'd be paid for my book review. I put it in the empty Bewley's tea tin, where we hid everything: food kitty and money for the gas stove.

Then Brigid told me she would be leaving before Easter, in eight weeks' time.

"You'll have a proper job by then," she added.

"You think so?"

"Yes. You have to be positive."

She had read *The Power of Positive Thinking* and applied its precepts to everything.

"Meantime, why not work part-time in the Claremont Inn?"

I'd been a chambermaid, a cinema usherette and a waitress one summer in London where I'd met Brigid, but had never worked in a pub. Brigid had had a job in the Claremont the previous summer, so knew the territory. It was a popular local pub and restaurant. They were always looking for help, and you could work a few hours at lunchtime, five days a week.

"It'll be impersonal," she said, "and you can still do your reviewing."

She never discouraged my freelancing. She just didn't like journalists.

Three

THE CLAREMONT TOOK me on. The hours weren't too challenging: 11 a.m. to 3 p.m. First I had to put the salads on a counter. Then, when the lunch customers started dribbling in at around noon, I took orders for the chef. He snapped my docket from a hatch in the wall and miraculously remembered everything, despite being a terrible grump. Chefs are often volatile. Nowadays I watch them sweating and swearing in sizzling TV kitchens from the safety of an armchair: even the calm ones blow up sometimes.

Amanda, the manageress, was a pill, too. Typically south Dublin, she was impeccably made up and wore a sort of bandana on her head, emphasizing Spanish looks. She must have been temporary, because she was too posh for a pub, but I never found out.

Lunch hour was hectic: all Ballsbridge seemed to descend on us with open mouths. I consoled myself that it left no time for self-pity. With waitressing and freelancing, I should make enough to get by. Declan's money would pay half the rent. Then, when Brigid left, I'd find someone for her room. I'd approach it systematically: advertise, put up notices in shops. It should be easy enough. Easter was over two months away, and I'd get used to life without her; you got used to anything. The new job was anonymous. I wouldn't know anyone among the banker types. I had a BA degree, but I'd ended up as a waitress. How had it happened?

And who appeared on my first day?

Nigel, my ex-boyfriend.

He came in the back door from the car park, laughing and talking. I couldn't believe it, but there he was, looking self-satisfied, as usual. A small, blond, neat person: his academic goatee beard had grown a bit. And he was wearing his best sports jacket and the grey lambswool sweater I had given him for his last birthday.

But the little fucker was with another woman! Already.

She didn't look his type. She was dowdy, a bluestocking with her hair in a bun, probably from the French department in Trinity. Was she living with him "full-time", as he had wanted me to do? While he scanned the room for a table from the edge of the lounge, I looked for signs of his rejuvenation. He hadn't seen me yet. But there was nowhere to hide, and I was hardly invisible. Why had he come to the Claremont? He had always lunched in the Buttery: healthy yoghurt and a sandwich. And he had never been one to splash out. At least, never on me.

They sat at one of my tables.

Damn.

I hoped Amanda would serve them, but after a few minutes she came over. "That couple are waiting."

I pretended not to understand. "Where?"

"Over there!"

"Oh."

"Take their order, Louise."

"Eh—could *you* possibly take it?"

"It's your table."

"I'm awfully busy."

"Take the order!"

"Please?"

"Take it!"

She stood there, so I had to go over.

"Hi, Nigel." I tried to look nonchalant.

He had the decency to redden. "Louise, what are you doing here?"

I gave him a dirty look. "Working."

"*Here?*"

"Yes." Where did he think?

"Eh . . . of course. Well, this is Hilly. From the history department."

I squirmed. He was describing me—as an ex-girlfriend, *I* was the history department. Although she looked too frumpy to last, and a Hilary, definitely a Hilary.

"Hi, Hilary."

"It's Hilly," Nigel insisted.

"Oh, sorry, Hilly. Hi, Hilly."

"Delighted to meet you." Her accent was English: polite and efficient.

I nodded curtly, as we shook hands.

"I've heard so much about you."

What did that mean? Nigel must have told her about me being useless in bed.

"Menu?" I shoved it at her, waiting with docket book in hand and wondering if Nigel would pay. He had always insisted on us going Dutch.

She had no right to *my* boyfriend but did I *really* want him? Brigid used to ask this in a scornful voice, because she had never liked Nigel. She always said he wasn't good to me, that I deserved better. And, anyway, how could I go out with a *Nigel?* He couldn't help his name, and the answer was *yes:* I did want him. He was a poor thing, but mine own. I had wanted to stand at the altar in a white dress and promise to be faithful till death did us part. My mother had been married with a child at my age, but I had blown things by my fear and frigidity. I wasn't modern, so he had gone off me. What was wrong with me?

Hilly studied the menu. "What's the pizza like?"

"Plastic," I said, although I didn't know.

She looked up, puzzled.

"I'm serious."

"Well, what do you recommend?"

"Nothing. There are specials—leftoverss—but I'd stay away from them."

Nigel gave me a suspicious look. "Leftovers?"

"Yes. Specials are always leftovers."

I hoped they would leave.

He looked alarmed. "I didn't know that."

"Except the salad bar," I added guiltily. "It's fresh. I laid it out."

"Laid it out?" Nigel talked as if it were a dead person on the table. He knew nothing about running a restaurant. How could he, coming from the privileged grove of Academe? He had gone to an English public school, then to Oxford, ending up with a First, while I had scraped through my degree.

I nodded. "*Put* it on the table."

Hilly smiled. "All by yourself?"

Was she joking? "Someone had to."

"Of course." She handed back the menu. "Well, I'll have that then."

"Me, too," Nigel piped up.

"The salad bar's self-service."

They only had to put it on a plate, yet they looked over helplessly.

"You make your *own* salad and take a docket from the table. It's all one price—no matter what you eat." This appealed to them, so I took the menus and left.

Amanda was behind me. "What did you say, Louise?"

I blinked. "Nothing."

"You said something about leftovers?"

Now I'd get the sack: the second time in two weeks.

"I said the food here was *better* than leftovers. That's what they'd be having at home."

She looked at me with disbelief. "You're here to *sell* food. This is a restaurant. The aim is to make money."

I felt my cheeks on fire. "I recommended the salad bar."

It was my first run-in with Amanda.

Nigel left without leaving a tip. I never discovered if he paid for Hilly. I didn't want to wait on them again. It was too painful. If the food was horrible, or I was horrible enough, maybe they would stay away. They'd stay in Trinity where they could butter each other up.

Four

I WAS BACK in the flat when the bell rang.

At first I ignored it and went on grappling with my review. Why did Tim give me boring books? It was hard to get through them, never mind think of something to say. A reviewer had to be dynamic, punchy, but I knew nothing about theology.

The bell went again.

I was in my dressing gown, so I didn't answer, thinking it might be a TV license inspector. Living in flatland, we had none.

Another sharp ring.

I peeped out the kitchen window: it was him, Peter the theologian. On the doorstep and dressed in a *priest's* uniform: black suit, white dog collar hidden by a grey wool scarf. His black hair was flattened down.

I opened the door, wanting to disappear. "Hello."

"Hi. Remember we met in Bernardo's?"

I nodded.

"Sorry—am I disturbing you?"

"No."

"You were in bed?"

"I'm working."

"In your robe?" He stared at my chest.

I checked that all was decent—no grubby bra straps. "It helps me concentrate."

"It does?"

"It's like drawing the blinds. I'm reviewing a book—about theologians."

"Perhaps I can help?"

He was still fixated by my breasts. I couldn't take my eyes off his collar.

"Why are you dressed like that?"

He looked surprised. "I'm a priest."

"Oh . . . the whole hog?"

He nodded.

I swallowed.

"It's the usual dress for a priest," he said.

"I thought you were in training. A novice or something."

"A novice?"

"You said you were *studying.*"

"Yes, but I'm ordained. I'm a Bernardite monk."

"Oh."

His eyes were blue, deeper than the ocean. I hadn't noticed the colour before. Now they searched mine.

"Remember Thursday?"

Jesus, could I ever forget it? Calling him a creep? Using the F word? Refusing to tell him where I lived? It all came back through a glass darkly, like bits of a bad dream. But there had been another feeling: when he put me to bed. That couldn't have been right, not with a priest.

"I made a holy show of myself."

He laughed. "You sure did."

"Yes."

"Well . . . how are you now?"

"Fine."

There was a pause.

"Thanks for bringing me home."

He smiled. "A pleasure. You Irish are great drinkers."

"I know."

"Three bottles of wine were brought to the table."

"Three?"

"I counted."

Another silence. He was staring at my breasts again.

"Eh . . . I must owe you for the taxi," I said.

"You don't."

"I must."

He shook his head, staring at the ground.

I searched for something else to say. "I should've rung . . . to thank you."

"That wasn't necessary." He looked up. "You *could* ask me in."

"Oh . . . but I'm working . . . and . . ." I pulled my dressing gown tight, "on my way to bed."

"I won't stay long."

"OK." I opened the door fully. "Come in for a coffee then."

As Peter came in and looked around curiously, I saw things through other eyes: despite our pride in it, our flat was grotty. As usual, the kitchen windows were fogged up. Half-full cups covered the white ring-marks on the dining room table. My stuff was all over it, as well as the typewriter. Newspapers littered the floor because I had been scouring the ads for a job. I'd planned to tidy up before Brigid got back from her sewing class. She was taking it in preparation for marriage. She was into self-improvement and spoke Irish.

"I see you type," he said, noticing the typewriter.

"I'm not very good."

"I'll need someone to type my thesis."

"That's highly specialised."

While I put the kettle on, he sat on the battered couch and flicked through the theology book. "An elementary introduction."

"OK, I'll say that."

"I see it has Hans Küng. My doctoral subject."

"He's a liberal, isn't he?"

"Yes, but he's irritated the pope. He's rejected papal infallibility."

"How can a human be infallible?"

"It's Catholic dogma. Küng wants to change too much."

"Isn't change good?"

"No. It has to come gradually."

"I'll work that in to the review."

"I'm a conservative. I hate the way they've messed up the Church. I entered because of the ritual."

"Incense and that sort of thing?" I should have been listening to all this, but I was looking for coffee. The cupboard was bare. "I'm afraid we're out of coffee. Will tea do?"

He shut the book. "Yes. Mind if I smoke?"

I did, but said no.

While the kettle boiled, he filled his pipe. "I ran into Dan Delaney yesterday. He was wondering how you were."

"I'm fine." The memory of the Lincoln Inn made me squirm.

"And Father Pat, another friend, said I should call down."

"He did?"

He lit up and exhaled a mushroom of smoke. "Yes. I was worried, so he said to pop in."

I peered through the smoke. "He did?"

"He thought I should check on how you were."

"I'm fine."

"See if you were all right."

"Oh."

"I had a responsibility—in the circumstances."

I laughed. "It took me a day or so. White wine's meant to be the worst hangover."

"It is?"

"Yes, it's meant to be."

"You're better then?"

I nodded.

"Lucky you didn't asphyxiate."

I coughed. "I've always been lucky."

A lie. We went on in this inane way, with him staring at my front. The gas ran out before the kettle boiled, so I searched for 10p coins in my bedroom. We still cooked in this pre-war way. Coin meters were everywhere in Dublin then. We had one for the phone, as well as for the gas and electricity.

Peter followed me, holding his pipe. "A cheery room."

I grabbed my underwear from the bed, hiding it under a pillow. My bedroom was north-facing, almost underground, since the back garden rose from a sunless moss-covered patio. But my new duvet was cheerful. The cover had purple flowers.

"The duvet's from Arnott's. They're all the rage now."

"What are?" Peter was staring again.

"Eh, duvets." I looked down; all was decent.

He quenched his pipe, pocketing it.

"You needn't waste time making the bed," I stammered. "And it's good for dust mites."

"Dust mites?" He gently touched my breast.

I pulled back, as my nipple jumped to life. "What are you doing?"

He looked embarrassed. "I don't know."

Small explosions went off inside me.

"Mites live on us. Disgusting, isn't it?"

He frowned. "Disgusting?"

"About dust mites—eating us?"

"I'm not sure."

What was he saying? It *was* disgusting, but before I could say anything else, he had started kissing me. I had never had such wavy feelings before.

"I wouldn't mind being a dust mite now," he whispered.

I was embarrassed. "Eh, would you mind stopping this?"

He carried on.

I pulled away. "I'm not on the pill."

He hesitated. "You're *not?"*

I shook my head.

"I thought everyone was nowadays."

"No."

I tried to push him away, but his hand was inside my bra. He caressed me until a depth charge went off inside me. Then he opened my dressing gown and removed my bra, staring at my breasts.

"My God, you're beautiful."

He was mad.

"Beautiful," he repeated.

I pulled on my dressing gown. "Will you please go?"

"I can't go now. Trust me."

I couldn't make him stop. We got all our clothes off and ended up making love under the purple flowers. With Peter, it was always a case of the nearest bed, and the first time was no exception.

Five

AFTERWARDS HE WAS in shock. We both were.

He pulled on his trousers, stumbling. "We'll have to forget this."

I nodded from the bed, wondering if Declan had heard us. He had come in and was in his bedroom. I knew by the loud punk music.

"I can't marry you," Peter said.

"I know."

"I'm a contemplative."

"What's that?"

"I've taken a vow of chastity."

Marry me? What was he talking about? He was the Good Samaritan who had saved me from the Outpatients or a Garda station. Maybe being arrested for disturbing the peace. It was an offence to be drunk in public. Only for him, I might have shouted rude things at someone else. How did that translate into marriage? And how the hell had we ended up in bed? I was the frigid type—that's what Nigel had called me—a guilty Catholic. Maybe I did think sex was a sin, deep-down. It had to be with a priest. But for some reason, I didn't feel sinful now.

"It was *meant* to be," Peter said when dressed.

"What do you mean?"

"Louise and Peter."

"So what?"

"You've heard of Héloïse and Abelard?"

"Is it a play?"

"Yes, but they were real people too."

"I remember now," I lied.

"Peter was a twelfth-century philosopher and she was his brilliant student."

"Well, the comparison ends there. I barely passed my degree."

He looked interested in this. "What subjects did you do?"

"English, history and philosophy."

"If you did philosophy, you should have heard of Abelard."

"He was a priest too?" I knew the name, but that was all.

"Yes, but later on. First he was a teacher. He had a child with Héloïse, so they got married, for which her family had him castrated."

"Jesus . . . that was a bit harsh."

Peter looked anxious, as he tightened his belt. "It was an honour thing."

I smiled. "You needn't worry about my family."

"That's a relief!"

"There's only my mother and brother. They're broad-minded."

"Héloïse went into a convent," he said.

"Luckily times have changed. I wouldn't like to be a nun."

"You don't have to be. But I've taken vows. Celibacy is still a rule of the Church."

He combed his hair at my mirror and put on his sheepskin overcoat. Then he came and knelt by my bed. He brushed my hair off my forehead, staring at me. "You're right out of Titian."

"I am?" I tried to remember his paintings, but none came to mind.

"We'll have to put this behind us."

I nodded again.

"We can have inter-subjectivity."

"What's that?"

"We can talk, but you'll have to understand the reality of the situation."

He went on talking about reality while stroking my hair. It seemed to fascinate him, as if it were the first he'd ever seen, like a Martian newly landed on earth. "Your hair's beautiful."

"It goes frizzy in the rain."

"You're a beautiful woman."

I laughed aloud. I was huge, size twelve, going on fourteen. I had a constant battle with my weight.

"I feel reborn, but I can't marry you."

"You've already said that."

"I have a vocation."

"Thou art Peter, and upon this rock, I will build my church," I said.

"That's right, love."

From the start, Peter was obsessed with marriage. How it wasn't for us. I thought of more mundane things: contraceptives for starters. There simply hadn't been time to get any. In Holy Catholic Ireland of the seventies, you couldn't buy them in a chemist even on prescription. Contraception was illegal and, like drug-taking, something you hid from your parents. You had to make a donation to the Family Planning Clinic and then be given a discreet brown paper parcel filled with condoms. Having no sex life, I had none in stock; and Peter, being a priest, didn't carry them around in his top pocket, ready for emergencies, as Nigel did. "Trust me" had meant trust his method of *coitus interruptus.*

The gas meter had got me into a fine mess.

"What about your tea?" I said in the hall. "I'll get change from the shop."

"No, love."

Peter kissed my forehead and we parted, vowing never to meet again.

I didn't go back to my review: my concentration was shattered. Instead I watched a university quiz on TV and thought about inter-subjectivity. Why hadn't I heard of it? And what if I was pregnant now? Oh God, my mother would be so upset. She was a romantic who liked *South Pacific*. Her idea of a girls' night out was *The Merry Widow*. This type of reality would shock her. How could I have done it to her? She, who had slaved to bring me up single-handedly. Her job in the Irish Hospital Sweepstakes paid a pittance, yet she had gone to work for years to feed ungrateful kids—that's my brother, William, and me.

Then the doorbell went again.

Nigel's Mini was at the gate.

God. What did he want?

I decided to hide.

He rang again, disturbing Declan, who came out in his sun-glasses.

"It's for me!" I said, running out to the hall.

"Sure, man." Declan went back to his room.

I opened the hall door. "Hi."

Nigel would guess about Peter, by looking at me. My hair was dishevelled, and sex must be written all over my face.

He was irritated. "Why didn't you answer the door?"

"I was asleep."

"So early?"

"I was tired. I fell asleep in front of the televison."

He had come for his Balzac novels, which took up half a shelf of the bookcase. I had meant to read them, but hadn't got round to it. After packing them into a box, he sauntered about, as if he still lived in the place. He had already taken his other possessions: the big radio, the toaster and the electric kettle. The turntable was mine, bought on the hire purchase. I only had one Bob Dylan record. All the others had been Nigel's.

Afterwards we had tea.

I watched as he scoffed all Brigid's oatmeal biscuits. She wouldn't be too pleased. She travelled with snacks to prevent her from fainting.

"You were odd with Hilly."

"It rhymes with silly. Silly Hilly."

He wagged a finger. "Now, now, don't be jealous."

"I'm not."

He smirked. "A pet name—which stuck."

"You're on *pet* terms pretty quickly." Then I hummed, "Hi Hilly, hi, Hilly, hi Ho! It's like Beethoven."

"That's not Beethoven!"

Nigel knew all about music, but I hated his superiority.

"You *are* jealous."

After Peter, how could I be? "No, honestly."

"You could've been friendlier to Hilly."

"I can't be friendly to everyone."

"It wouldn't have hurt."

I said nothing.

His tone softened, as he picked the last apple from the bowl. "Are you feeling better?"

Did he know about Peter? Could he read my mind?

"What do you mean?"

"I saw you in a bad state—Monday afternoon?"

"Oh, that . . ."

"You were coming out of the pub as I was driving into Trinity."

I tried to laugh it off. "Yes . . . I got a terrible hangover."

Dublin was like that—a village. It was impossible to keep secrets. When I told him about Tim's lunch, he shook his head.

"You've cooked your goose now."

"What do you mean?"

"You've ruined your reputation."

I made a face. Did he think it was the Middle Ages?

"That guy you were with could've raped you."

What he was saying was ridiculous. And it sounded as if he *knew,* but he couldn't have.

"He's a theologian."

He sighed. "Even worse."

"Look, you may have a one-track mind, but—"

"I'm concerned for you."

"Well, don't be!" I wanted to get off the subject. Was there a mark on my forehead, like Cain?

"*I* know you, but people might think things."

He didn't know me.

He smiled again. "You can't help being a good little Catholic."

So that's what he thought about my failures. Well, maybe it was *his* fault. Had he ever thought that he hadn't done it *right? With* nipples, rather than *without?* It had worked with Peter. Why was that?

He sighed. "Tim'll never employ you now."

"He already does."

"I mean full-time. That job you applied for."

I didn't say it had gone to the ex-cleric. "I'm not the first person in the world to get drunk."

"It's always worse in a woman."

"What's worse?"

"Alcoholism. Think of your mother."

That's what I got for confiding in him. Of course, my mother hadn't helped by ringing him up one day when she'd had a few and telling him to hurry up and marry me, or she'd complain about him to the provost. No wonder he had broken it off. Anyone could become an alcoholic—my mother had after my father's death. I hardly qualified, but couldn't defend myself: I was too upset. I just watched as Nigel remembered other stuff: the teapot and the pyrex dish for roasting chickens—that was in the old days when we could afford food. Nowadays we lived on Brigid's greasy cabbage, or beans and rice. Why hadn't I hidden the dish? How would we cook now?

He poked in the cupboard. "Mind if I take my mugs?"

"No."

How had our holiday souvenirs become *his?* They were *ours,* something for the bottom drawer. I had always thought so. Did it matter who paid for what?

After denuding us, Nigel left. Mugs didn't matter, and he mattered even less. It was sad, but true. Later, as I was going to bed, the phone rang. At first, I ignored it, thinking it might be my mother.

It was Peter.

"Why didn't you answer?"

"I didn't know it was you."

So we devised a secret method: he would ring twice, hang up, then ring back.

"I feel reborn," he said finally, "but I can't see you again."

"No."

"Sleep well."

"I'll try."

He hung up, and I was awake all that night.

It's hard to know why things happen. I mean our affair, of course. Maybe it was the kindness of strangers. Or something to do with my sad childhood and all that psychological stuff? My father dying young? Breaking up with Nigel? But you can't blame others for your fate. I was old enough to know that sex with a priest was wrong. My mother would now have a reason to go back on the bottle. She'd have something to tell everyone: my *terrible* daughter. My brother, William, had predicted my downfall, too. He was a typical older brother. I was twenty-five, without a job, and bedding a Cistercian offshoot. It sounded like something from a gardening manual.

Six

THE NEXT DAY I went to work in a trance.

I even smiled at Amanda, who made me clean the ashtrays. The world had taken on an aura. How had it happened so quickly? All the metaphysical poetry I had slogged through in college now made sense. *"Who ever loved that loved not at first sight?"* Who had written that? It sounded like Herbert, but I couldn't discover when I looked it up. *"Love bade me welcome: yet my soul drew back, / Guilty of dust and sin."* That was definitely Herbert.

Overnight my failures with Nigel faded into a memory. I now had a real problem. I hadn't taken any vows of celibacy. I wasn't religious at all, but a lapsed Catholic, while Peter was chosen by God to do great things with his life. I'd seen him across a crowded room, yet had known him all my life. We had been born for each other. Love was the candle in the dark, the light that led us on. It was something we all hoped for.

Yet hope for Peter was hopeless. I knew that.

And the thought of not seeing him again was terrible.

I needn't have worried. He was sitting on my windowsill after work the next afternoon, reading a book by Hans Küng. Beside him was a guitar case.

I took him into my bedroom, because there was music coming from Declan's room. He was a follower of David Bowie and a new London band, the Sex Pistols, whose music he played all the time. I was a late developer and didn't know about bands, only things like Dylan and Simon and Garfunkel and bridges over troubled water, which was something I needed now.

Peter put his arms around me.

I pulled back. "Maybe we shouldn't?"

He kissed me. "Give me chastity, but not yet."

I laughed. "Who said that?"

"Saint Augustine. Have you read his *Confessions?*"

"No." I didn't know what he was talking about.

"It's an autobiography. I'll get you a copy."

"Listen, I'll make tea. I have biscuits."

He kissed me in reply.

"We shouldn't be doing this," I said, as he touched my face. "Not without contraceptives."

Peter didn't say anything, and the next thing we were in bed. He caressed me with the same consequences, and we made love for a second time. Again it was an explosion that I had never experienced before. This was how love was meant to be: people killed for it, died for it. Every song in the world was about it, and nearly every poem.

Afterwards Peter was in despair again.

He sat on the edge of the bed, pulling on his clothes. "I was propositioned."

I was puzzled. "I wish you hadn't said that."

Cary Grant had used the word "propositioned" to Eve Marie Saint in Hitchcock's *North by Northwest,* when they met on the train. It had been on television over Christmas and was full of romantic dialogue. I had watched it with my mother, who liked old movies. But I didn't think Peter was being romantic now. He looked deadly serious. "Propositioned" was not in my vocabulary, and even in the film, Cary Grant's use of it had puzzled me. I knew prostitutes propositioned for sex, but what was Peter saying? Did he look on me like that? A fallen woman who had snared him. A Magdalene? Another Eve, who had eaten the apple?

He repeated the word. "I was propositioned by your looks."

I threw my shoe at him. "Don't say that word! I can't help my looks!"

He ducked. "You shouldn't be allowed out."

"You shouldn't come here! What am I to do when you touch me? I—I love you."

"That's a big word, Louise."

I threw another shoe. Then a book. He jumped out of the bed, grabbed my arm. "Stop shouting! Someone will hear!"

Declan's music had stopped, but I didn't care. "You're hurting me."

"Stop throwing things."

"Admit you came here. I didn't run after you."

He wouldn't let me go.

"Admit it!"

"Be quiet."

"I won't! Admit you came here—uninvited."

At last he said, "Yes, I did."

I was crying. "Well, *say* it!"

"I *came* here."

"Uninvited!"

"I came uninvited."

There were tears in his voice too. It was our first quarrel.

He let me go and started picking up the shoes. "I didn't know you were violent."

"Well, I am. You're never to touch me again."

"It'd be easy to break it off with you now, Louise."

"That'd be great if you did."

This threw him. He finished dressing and stood there, looking at me.

I had pulled on my blouse and trousers. "What are you waiting for?"

"I don't know."

"Just go, and don't come back!"

"You're throwing me out?"

"I am!"

"Now—"

"Please go!"

He held my shoulders. "Look at me."

"No!"

"I was waiting for you . . . because I can't live without you. I think about you every minute of every day. I—I love you too."

I stopped crying and he handed me a tissue. I should have held out for a real apology that first time. But those words *"I love you"* cut a hole in my heart. Looking back, it was because I had never heard them from a man, and it seemed I had been waiting for them all my life. So we made up and went back to bed, lying in each other's arms. Afterwards he played a piece of guitar music he was learning. It was beautiful and by someone I'd never heard of.

When Declan went out, we went into the sitting room for a cup of tea.

"If only we'd met before I was ordained," Peter filled his pipe, as I put on the kettle, "things might have been different."

"When were you ordained?"

He lit up. "Last November."

I was two months late.

"You could still leave. Priests do these days."

"I can't marry you."

"*Stop* saying that!"

"You have to understand the reality of the situation."

"You're using clichés."

"Nonetheless, it's true."

Peter frowned over his pipe. The room had filled with smoke, smelling of vanilla and old leather. "I can never even see you again."

Again I agreed.

"Never," he repeated, biting the stem of his pipe.

He was right: our love was impossible. His hands had been anointed. *Noli me tangere* was a favourite expression. And he had been in touch with God through meditation. At least, that's what he told me, and I was a temptress, a siren, luring him to destruction. We couldn't be seen together, never mind go to the cinema or anything ambitious like that. But I certainly wasn't becoming a nun. He could forget that idea. So, after tea, we parted for the third time.

"What's wrong, darling?"

My mother sat at the other side of the table. I was home in Ranelagh for Sunday lunch, in the chilly dining room of my childhood home, a terraced house, oozing red-bricked respectability. Nothing in it had changed since my father's death: the same dreary paintings looked down from the walls; the armchairs where he had read the paper after work had got lumpier; the Persian carpet was more threadbare. In the sideboard were the Waterford glasses, my parents' unused wedding presents. The only additions were graduation photos of William and me, on top. I was all my mother had now, because my brother had emigrated to London. According to her, he got all the brains owing to a craving for oysters when she was pregnant with him. I'd been the product of a passion for grapes.

"Nothing." I stared at her rubbery lasagne. "Nothing's wrong."

I was aching to tell her about Peter, but couldn't.

My mother was a faded beauty, dark and blue-eyed. Now her eyes were anxious and her grey roots were showing. She should have had her hair done professionally, but did it at home to save money. Otherwise she still had a lovely figure. It was sad that she hadn't remarried. My father had been gone for fifteen years. That meant that she had been widowed with two children in her early thirties, only eight years older than I was now.

"You don't look well," my mother persisted.

"I'm fine."

"You're pale."

Her X-ray eyes would see through me.

If Brigid had been shocked by Peter, what would my mother's reaction be? She was only forty-eight and a liberal, except in her attitude to her children. William and I had to succeed, to make up for her hardships. She'd been through years of struggle in a time of drab depression during the Irish forties and fifties. Yet maybe she would understand; she had had her own liaisons down the years. Although she had never replaced my father, she had got by through a series of unattainable crushes on my brother's headmasters: priests or Christian Brothers. At the moment she was friendly with Canon FitzSimon, our ex-parish priest, but I didn't suspect anything there, because he was a distant relative of my father's. She had no one else to talk to, so I had been her confidante from a young age, but Brigid had warned me not to tell her about my latest "boyfriend". It would worry her too much, and my mother was frail. Any stress might tip her off the wagon.

"You're not eating anything."

"I am." I pushed my fork around the plate.

"I went to great trouble to do something new."

"It's delicious."

Lasagne was her latest attempt at avant-garde living—which said something about our family. The dish was over-herbed, but cooking wasn't everyone's thing. As a child, I'd had nothing to compare my mother's to, so I thought it was OK, since she always said it was. I had usually managed to eat her efforts, but since Peter, I had lost my appetite. I'd lost weight too, which was great. I was under ten stone again.

During the apple tart, my mother said, "Want to tell me about it?"

I shook my head.

My mother had been off drink for years, so I usually confided in her. I suppose we were intimate because of my father. Sorrow binds people or else does the opposite. In our case it bound. I had told her all about breaking up with Nigel. She had been sympathetic then, but said she wasn't sorry: I might have had to live in England. She had pretended not to care, although she secretly wanted me settled in life. If I had married Nigel, she could have worn a big floppy hat to the wedding and bought a new dress as the mother of the bride. The ceremony would have been in University Church, too, which she would have loved. She read the social and personal columns of *The Irish Times* every Saturday, keeping track of my schoolfriends' engagements. She had wanted mine printed there: *Mrs Maureen O'Neill, widow of the late Michael O'Neill of Ranelagh, is happy to announce the engagement of their only daughter, Louise, to Nigel, son of Mr and Mrs Swales of Birmingham, England.*

I had deprived her of that, although she hadn't helped with her phone calls.

For that reason, I didn't want to tell her about Peter, but she knew something was wrong.

The next morning I got condoms from the Family Planning Clinic. I wasn't taking any more chances. If I wasn't strong enough to resist Peter, I would protect myself from pregnancy at least. That afternoon, he was back on my windowsill, reading the same book. He had already tried to get in the window, but Brigid had locked it because she worried about burglars.

We went in and I put on the kettle. He took several books from his duffle bag: *To Be a Pilgrim, Confessions of Saint Augustine* and *The Brothers Karamazov.* Also a bottle of wine and several bottles of Guinness from the monastery cellars.

"Thanks," I said, "but I don't think you should stay."

His blue eyes were worried. "Have you had your period?"

I went red. "It isn't due yet."

"When did you last have it?"

I refused to answer. Why didn't he shut up?

"Please, Louise, I'm worried about you."

"It's every twenty-eight days. I'm somewhere in the middle."

It was embarrassing talking about such things. But Peter knew all about female bodily functions. Unlike Irish priests, he hadn't entered the monastery after school. He hadn't even been raised Catholic, but had converted sometime in his teens to the Roman Catholic Church—he always called himself a *Roman* Catholic, whereas in Ireland we were merely Catholic. His childhood had been unhappy—his mother had died when he was four. Then he had had a career in the business world: an accountancy firm in Toronto of all things. There had been a full-time mistress: her name had been Stella, and she had run a leg-waxing business. The day God had called, he had been at the races and had just lost a fortune on a horse. Afterwards he was in the bar, feeling miserable, when he'd been hit with his Damascene moment. Soon afterwards, he had gone to Alberta and entered the strictest monastery he could find to make up for a life of wine, women and racehorses. To everyone's surprise, he became a brilliant student and qualified for a higher degree. His order paid the fees.

He kissed me, but I resisted, remembering the last time.

"What is it?"

"I don't think we should."

"Oh, Louise."

"Last time you said something."

He frowned. "What did I say?"

"You used a certain word."

"What word?"

"Propositioned—you're pretending to forget."

"I'm sorry, Louise. I didn't mean it."

"Then why did you say it?"

"Because I felt guilty. Young women are so beautiful."

"Now you're talking rot."

He tried to kiss me again, but I held out.

"We shouldn't be doing this."

He looked miserable. "I know."

"Well, *one* more time then—if you use these." I pulled out my packet of condoms.

He put them on the table. "I can't use rubbers."

"But . . ."

"You'll have to trust me."

"What if something happens?"

"It won't."

"I told you, I'm in the middle of my cycle."

"I won't go all the way."

"Promise you'll leave then?" I said.

"I promise."

"For good?"

"Yes."

"You won't come back?"

He agreed, so we went to bed, where he performed his usual trick of withdrawing at the last minute. As he was pulling on his trousers afterwards, I asked how he could say mass in the morning. Wasn't it a sin?

"I'll go to confession," he said.

"You confess and it's OK?"

"That's the general idea."

Then Peter told me he had already confessed our affair to his best friend, another priest called Father Pat, the one who had sent him down to check that I was still breathing after I'd over-imbibed in Bernardo's.

"I was expecting a stiff penance, but he asked me to hear his confession. He has a woman friend."

"He's having an affair, too?"

"No, he has a woman *friend.*"

"He told you that in confession?"

He looked cross. "Didn't you learn anything in school?"

"I did."

"Then you should know about the seal of confession. He told me *as a friend.* Not in confession."

"Oh."

"He can't marry because of his vocation to the missions."

"Couldn't they go on the missions as a couple? For Concern? Or Oxfam?"

"He wouldn't be able to say mass."

"What's so special about saying mass?"

Peter looked sad. "I shouldn't be surprised that you don't understand. You're not a Catholic, Louise."

"I'm baptised."

"You're not practising. You couldn't understand the seriousness of a vocation."

I did understand: I was getting experience at first hand. Peter had another life unshared with me: the university and his role in a religious community where he had the duties of a priest. He never stayed over because it was against the monastery rules, but I imagined that if he did, we would wake in the dark and make love again. After he left that day, the sadness of celibacy made me cry. Yet I envied Peter's calling: I wanted one myself, although not for religion. If only I could do something serious, instead of freelancing for a right-wing rag. I decided to change my life and signed up for musical appreciation classes in the local tech, which were beginning after Easter. I would become good at something. I started reading Dostoevsky and poetry, especially Blake's "Garden of Love".

I went to the Garden of Love,
And saw what I never had seen:
A Chapel was built in the midst,
Where I used to play on the green.

It was dead-on.

I read it to Peter, who listened without commenting. He didn't know anything about Blake, so I bought him a poster of *Ancient of Days,* Blake's depiction of God as an architect. In return, he gave me the poems of St John of the Cross, which explained his love of God.

In search of my Love,
I will go over mountains and strands;
I will gather no flowers,
I will fear no wild beasts;
And pass by the mighty and frontiers.

Seven

THE FLAT BEGAN to rock with music and reek of marijuana. Declan played tapes non-stop. He had dropped out of Trinity and was trying to become a pop star, so he stayed home all day writing lyrics in the style of David Bowie or Lou Reed. This was awkward. I dreaded him discovering that Peter was a priest. It was probably paranoid. Not that Declan would be scandalised or anything, being a practising heathen, but I didn't want it getting round Trinity, because then Nigel might hear. So far I had managed to keep them apart, although, despite his resolutions, Peter appeared almost every afternoon. He played the guitar in my bedroom, so I told Declan he was giving me music lessons. They had met only once, by accident in the dark, when Peter was sneaking out of my bedroom and Declan was on the way to the bathroom. Otherwise, Declan stayed in his room with the door closed, so he didn't notice anything to approve or disapprove of. He came out only at night, slinking around like a cat.

I assumed he was smoking pot full-time, but I learnt otherwise.

His girlfriend, Clothilde, a French *au pair,* was always around. She even slept over illegally. I hadn't said anything because of Peter visiting. Besides, I liked Clothilde: she spoke French to me and said my accent was good. I even learnt to curse in French. But Brigid felt invaded by her, saying Clothilde was always in front of the TV when she came home from school and wanted to mark copy books. Then she watched us eating, so we had to offer her food. "Declan's only paying for one," Brigid would whisper to me, "and, have you noticed? He steals our food."

I had, although I had lost all interest in eating. Declan never bought anything but Coke and Mars Bars, which he had for breakfast. Sometimes he'd cook a mountain of spuds for his dinner, leaving the skins everywhere. He stole all our coffee, too, and never cleaned up: the fridge was full of wilting lettuce and sour milk.

Then something happened: Brigid and I were cooking in the kitchen when we heard screams. At first I thought it was Declan's tapes—David Bowie gone mad, the Sex Pistols, or some band of unknown screamers coming from his bedroom—but the screams were real. Even though we had the TV on, we still heard them. It was Clothilde.

After the sound of slapping, we heard Declan curse. He was fond of swearing in the middle of sex. Sometimes he shouted the c-word. Then some other word I didn't understand.

I looked at Brigid. "Is it Russian?"

She shook her head, turning up the TV.

But the slapping and screams rose to a crescendo with the unmistakable sound of the bed squeaking rhythmically. Violent sex horrified us, but Brigid and I were too shocked to say anything that first time, although Clothilde had a black eye. To me it was worse than Peter being a priest, and we both worried about her since she was still in her teens. Had she got into the clutches of a sadist? Or did she think it was an Irish sexual custom to batter a woman? You read about people like Declan, but meeting one was another thing.

We were too embarrassed to say anything that time, but during another noisy session Brigid said, "That's it! He's leaving, and she has to go immediately!"

We decided to deal with Declan later, but as soon as Clothilde came out of the bedroom, we planned to call a taxi, telling her it wasn't fair to crowd us out. It got late and in the end Brigid went to bed. Unlike me, she had to get up in the morning. I was designated to perform the eviction, so I waited up in the sitting room. At last Clothilde crept through to the kitchen to make tea for herself and Declan. Her hair was dishevelled and her mascara messy. Seeing me, she was embarrassed.

There was something vulnerable about her. Instead of being firm, I asked if she was OK.

She looked at the floor. "What you mean?"

"You know what I mean."

"No."

"We hear things, Brigid and I."

She tried to bluff it out. "What you hear?"

"Shouting."

"Shouting?"

I persisted. "Declan hits you."

"No."

"Yes?"

She started to cry. "He no like tame love."

"Do you agree to it?"

"I no understand."

"You want the hitting?"

"The hit-*ting?*"

"Violence. Declan hits you."

"I like Declan, not hits."

"Well then, you don't have to put up with it."

"I no do?" She wiped her eyes, smudging the mascara even more. Then held up a bruised arm. "He hit here."

"God!" It was a big black bruise. "Tell him to stop it!" I sat her down and made a cup of tea. "Do you want me to speak to him?"

"No, *please* not."

So I ended up sharing her tea, instead of calling a taxi and sending her home. Apparently Declan had persuaded her this was sex Irish-style, so I was determined to speak to him. Because he was in bed all day, this wasn't easy. The next weekend he threw a party, filling the flat with loud Trinity students. It drove Brigid wild. Long-haired girls and boys spread themselves around the front room, sitting on cushions and smoking pot. We had been invited at the last minute and went reluctantly, trying the noxious vegetarian concoction—brown rice and bean stodge. It had kept him up the night before and taken up the whole kitchen to cook. There had been a row when Brigid made him clean up.

The party got into full swing, but wine and water did not mix. We were older, different types as well. We stood around, awkwardly sipping wine. A tall girl in a mini laughed hysterically because Brigid was a teacher and I worked for *The Catholic Trumpet.*

"We have a writer from *The Catholic Trumpet!*" she yelled across the room.

I didn't know if it was drink or drugs.

In the end we retreated to our beds, but sleep was impossible. All night punk rock screeched from my turntable, which had been borrowed without permission. At three in the morning, Brigid knocked on my door.

"You awake, Louise?"

I let her in.

"We'll have to throw them out or be evicted ourselves," she whispered.

That was true. The landlady might have called the guards already. We went into the sitting room in our dressing gowns and saw bodies strewn everywhere. There was a smell of cigarettes and pot. Empty beer bottles, drained bottles of cheap cider and Hirondelle wine covered the table. A couple were embracing intimately on the couch. Everyone was stoned.

Brigid turned off the music and went round shaking people. "Wakey-wakey. Time to go home."

Most wouldn't move. A few looked up, bleary-eyed.

"Time, everyone!" I pretended to be a barman. "The party's over."

A boy opened his eyes.

"Time to go home," I repeated.

"I've missed the last bus," he mumbled, going back to sleep.

What was he talking about? They had come *afte*r the last bus. Buses had never been in the picture. They'd have to call taxis, several taxis.

No one would budge.

Brigid knocked on Declan's door.

No answer.

She used her schoolteacher voice. "Declan, I know you're in there."

Still, no answer.

"Is Clothilde with you?"

Nothing.

"Louise and I want your friends to go. Now!"

No answer.

Brigid rapped on the door. "Clothilde is not allowed sleep here."

She tried the door, but it was locked. "Tell your friends to go!"

Then we got a sleepy answer. "Man, they can't go now."

"They have to!"

"Cool it, man."

Brigid rattled the handle. "Declan, open this door!"

He wouldn't, so in the end, we went back to bed.

The next morning, Brigid threw out the remaining bodies. Then she knocked on Declan's door again.

At first he pretended to be asleep.

"You're on your last chance," she said. "Louise backs me up."

I stood behind her. "Yes, I do. And stop abusing Clothilde."

At last I had said it.

He peeped out, wearing only black underpants and John Lennon shades. "There are house rules," Brigid said. "From now on, you'll have to obey them or leave."

"Cool it, man. You're overreacting."

Brigid was red in the face. "You're not to invite anyone here without permission. Clothilde's in there, isn't she?"

"It's none of your business."

She stood her ground. "You can't have women staying over."

"And you're to stop hitting her," I added.

"Don't be so bloody bourgeois." He looked past Brigid to me. "Louise lets Peter in her room."

"He never stays the night," I said.

Brigid supported me. "No, he doesn't. Clothilde is to sleep in her own place from now on."

Declan grinned, and gave a Nazi salute. "Heil, ma'am!"

Brigid was really angry now. "If you have another party without our permission, you're out!"

He slammed the door in our faces and put on more deafening music.

The landlady *had* to have heard the party. She *must* have smelt Declan's marijuana coming up through the floorboards. It went everywhere, even out into the road. Or else she'd heard his girlfriend screaming. Would we be evicted because of them, out on the side of the road for running an S&M club? Just in case, we avoided Miss Pym, ducking in and out of the flat when we knew she wouldn't be in the front garden. Although the violent sex stopped, Clothilde never thanked me for intervening on her behalf. Despite the warning, Declan still let her stay over. We knew she was in there, but couldn't prove it because his curtains were always drawn and the door kept shut. The curtains alone were enough to freak the landlady. We couldn't ban visitors, because Brigid's fiancé came for weekends. And, of course, Peter was always there. Brigid guessed what was going on with him and disapproved, but I felt she was being unfair and judgemental. Just as she had hated Nigel and his trendy Mini, she now disliked Peter without knowing him. He couldn't help his vocation, or his feelings for me.

"Your mother rang," Brigid said one day.

I was making chilli. "Thanks."

I had avoided her phone calls and had only been home once since meeting Peter.

"Are you going to ring her back?"

"I suppose."

"What'll she think of your man?"

"Peter? Oh, she's pretty liberal."

Brigid humphed. "She'd need to be."

"What do you mean?"

"It's a real surprise—you going with a priest and all."

"I know."

"You should end it."

"I tried. He can't live without me."

"That's rubbish."

"We're in love, Brigid."

"It won't come to anything." She stared at me, puzzled. "I've never had that feeling. Not *once* in all my life."

I was shocked. "But you love Sam?"

"I'd have no interest if he wasn't marrying me."

That was Brigid. I pitied her lack of feeling. But she was right: I wasn't the religious type and my actions puzzled me too. How had it happened? It had to be my childhood. I was a well of insecurity from my father's loss and my mother's drinking.

In the Ireland of the day, there was no place for Peter and me. There still wouldn't be, although it might be more accepted now. That's what people tell me, thirty years on. Then there was nowhere to go. Maybe if there had been, we wouldn't have been so intense. We had to stay in my bedroom, where the inevitable happened. Sometimes Peter played his classical guitar, and sometimes we watched old films on TV. Otherwise we visited Peter's friends. When Clinton was elected in America and people came out of the woodwork as FOBs (Friends of Bill), I was reminded of Peter's friends—FOPs. These varied from a Church of Ireland clergyman, with whom he had ecumenical discussions, to a semi-famous artist. He was friendly with a couple of middle-aged ladies from the Canadian embassy, and a sick older woman who lived way out in the suburbs was on his regular visiting list. I forget her name, but she had been at Peter's ordination and doted on him as a son. He brought me to meet her, warning me in the bus not to use any bad language. I was careful, noticing the old woman's unhealthy colour and wheezy breathing. Because of her bad health, her daughter had cooked our meal of fillet steak.

Peter was gentle with her, and I saw a new side to him. He was a priest, visiting someone in need. I was preventing him from doing his job. We would have to break up.

"You shouldn't have gone to this trouble," he scolded, although his eyes were soft.

"I didn't go to any trouble." The old woman wheezed, turning to me. "That monastery food is terrible. He needs someone to mind him."

Peter laughed, so I supposed it must be true about the food. Afterwards, when he went to the bathroom, she stared at me for a few seconds. "I hope you're being minded, too."

I didn't know what to say.

What did she mean by that? Did she know about us?

Eight

OUR NEXT "DATE" was dinner with a German family. Heiner, a friend of Peter's, lived with his wife and six strapping children in a big house on the Sidmonton Road in Bray. The trains were infrequent then, so we took the 45 bus. We sat upstairs on the front seat, as the double-decker brushed the treetops. I became nauseous from the rocky motion, as we careered along the old Bray road like the last stage to Santa Fe.

Instead of being sympathic, Peter was horrified. "You're sick?"

I nodded miserably.

"Oh, my God!"

"What?"

"You're pregnant?"

I shook my head. "I'm always sick on a bus."

He kept groaning. "It's morning sickness."

"This is the *afternoon.*"

He looked as if he'd burst. "I know you're pregnant."

"I'm not! If I were, it'd be too soon for morning sickness. Now shut up, please."

"Louise, show some respect. Behave yourself."

"*You* behave yourself."

This annoyed him, and we fell into silence as the bus neared Bray.

"If you're so worried about pregnancy, why don't you use a contraceptive?" I said.

"I shouldn't expect you to understand." Then he repeated his accusation. "You're not a practising Catholic."

"I'm an *Irish* Catholic."

"No, you're not even Christian."

I wasn't a proper Catholic because I didn't go to mass and wanted to use a contraceptive. Now I wasn't a Christian either. It irked me, because I tried to be kind: to love others as myself. The trouble was I didn't love myself. I was too much of a mess.

Peter was wearing his work clothes again: black suit and white dog collar. He looked on the priest's uniform as a sort of armour, I had decided, the way knights long ago wore breastplates in battle. He thought the colour black would protect him from me.

His accusations always made me defensive.

"I suppose you're a Christian because you're dressed up."

"I'm not dressed up."

"Then why not dress like everyone else?"

"I belong to a religious order."

"Well, I'm a bloody Christian."

"Don't blaspheme."

"I'm not!"

"A Christian is a follower of Jesus Christ."

I didn't want to quarrel, so said nothing more. I had been christened Louise *Christine,* which meant "the anointed one". I had been baptised and gone to a Catholic school.

"I can't help having no faith," I said after a bit.

Peter softened. "It's a gift. Not given to everyone."

"How come you got it?"

"Louise, you have to open your heart, invite Him in. I can tell you one thing: if you ever did, it'd blow your mind."

"Why do you say that?"

"You're the most passionate person I've ever met. You have great spiritual depths, but you leave them untouched."

My experience of religion had been rosaries and dreary school retreats. It had been nothing to do with passion, which so far I had felt only for poetry and some novels. But now I felt for Peter.

At Bray the bus turned left by the hotel, crossed the railway line and tore along the sea front.

Peter broke the silence. "I love it when you wash your hair."

I tried to be sensible. "You're not meant to say that."

"I can't help it."

"You can," I whispered. "You can *stop*."

"You're a beautiful woman, and I can't help loving you."

"Oh, shut up!"

"Louise!"

I looked round. What if someone heard? Why was he so reckless in public? Luckily the woman in the back of the bus was bent over a newspaper.

When we got off, the tide was out, and seaweed was strewn on the beach. I wondered if this was symbolic: time running out on our love. We walked up from the sea front to a residential road with big houses and old, leafless trees. Peter flattered and puzzled me at the same time. No one had ever said things about my hair and body, and me being beautiful. I don't think Nigel had ever paid me a compliment in our two years together. To him I was stupid. I had no hope of being an academic, and that was all he cared about—"us academics". But Peter had said I was passionate, so our relationship must be love. It made you see things in coloured light, only it distorted your vision. Peter was macho, yet I forgave him. And he thought I was sexually liberated, so I became so with him. Were we just other people's projections?

We stopped outside a big Victorian house. A wintry vine grew up the red-bricked front, and there were bay windows with interesting Romeo and Juliet balconies.

Peter opened the gate. "I want no bad language here."

"I don't use bad language."

"You've a mouth like a sailor. You said *bloody* on the bus."

"It's the vernacular."

"These people are respectable."

Before I could argue, our host, Heiner, appeared and let us in to a dark hall full of dreary paintings and ugly mahogany furniture. He was one of those old-fashioned conservative Catholics who had escaped to Ireland in the Nazi era. Peter told me he had been hidden for months in a Bavarian monastery. He'd built up a business in Ireland and had got rich from making screws or bolts for the insides of cars. Like Peter, he preferred the Latin mass and had some connection with the monastery. It must have been financial, because he was so rich, or maybe gratitude for his escape.

He was portly and bald and shook my hand too hard. "Velcome, my dear."

His wife, Johanna, stood behind him, beaming. She was a frau-type with a Scottish kilt and a sensible bun like Hilly's. "Ja, velcome."

Heiner gave us sherry in the chintzy drawing-room, while Johanna disappeared to the kitchen to see to the dinner. Then the tribe of children filed in. They varied in age: small, teenaged, and twenty-something girls, all blonde and beautiful. The little ones were dressed alike, so that I expected them to burst into song, like the Trapp family. The eldest was around my age and had just qualified in medicine. I wondered what she thought of me? Did she think it funny me being with Peter? We must have looked an odd couple.

As I talked to her, the younger sisters chatted to Peter. Their lisping accents floated over: "Father, when are you returning to Canada?" "Have you been on holidays yet?" Again, I saw him in another light. To them, he was *Father* Peter, and they obviously liked him and knew him well from previous visits. He glowed with the attention, glancing worriedly over at me. Did he think I was revealing anything? Well, I wasn't. No, I was pretending to be interested in boring medicine.

Before dinner, I went upstairs to the loo. It was a huge old-fashioned bathroom with an antique tub and gold taps. The toilet was on a kind of throne. I was washing my hands, wondering if the taps were real gold, when I heard Peter outside.

"Louise?"

"What is it?"

"Open the door."

I peeped from behind it. "What?"

"I have to hold you."

I shut the door in his face.

I waited for a while, thinking he had tiptoed back down the stairs, but as I came out, he pushed me back into the bathroom. We ended up with me sitting on the side of the tub and almost falling in backwards.

I struggled free.

"I love you, Louise."

"Stop it! They'll hear!"

"I can't help it."

"They might come upstairs. What'll they think?"

"I don't care what anyone thinks."

"You'll be giving scandal. To the children!"

He pulled back. "You're right."

I left him in the bathroom and went ahead down the stairs. To my alarm, he followed me, touching my behind and breathing heavily. I hit his hand off, but it was useless. He stopped this behaviour near the end, but there were a few curious stares as we reached the hall where the family were now filing into the dining room in order of age, the youngest first. At first I imagined they must know what had happened, but they couldn't have guessed anything, because they went on chatting happily to each other, as we took our allotted places at a long dark mahogany table, laden with two types of glasses and all the right cutlery.

Peter had recovered his composure.

He bowed his head. "Now we'll sing grace."

The family began singing to the tune of "Edelweiss":

Bless our friends, bless our food,
Come O Lord, and sit with us.
May our talk glow with peace
Bring your love to surround us.
Friendship and peace.
May they bloom and grow
Bloom and grow for ever.
Bless our friends, bless our food,
Bless our sharing together.

They *were* the Trapp family. My mother would have been in heaven.

As Peter said another prayer, I studied the family's concentrated faces. What would they think of us sleeping together? Everyone would be so shocked. And I'd be the sinner, when Peter had started everything and carried on like a lunatic. He talked rubbish about being a contemplative, when all he wanted was to bed me. But I went along with it, like some sort of hypnotised person. What was wrong with me? Brigid was right—I'd have to give him up. We couldn't go on like this.

There was wine for the adults and milk for the children. The soup was in a huge tureen, from which Johanna served. Croutons to float in it were passed round. Then came the main course of vegetables, meat and roast potatoes. I'll always remember the roast beef: a tender cut, which I afterwards discovered was rib roast. It was my first time to taste it. I'd only had stringy housekeeper's cut before—every Sunday of my life. My mother prided herself as a cook, but her meat always turned into grey leather, like the boots Charlie Chaplin cooked in that film where he had dinner in a cabin with the big fat man.

Everyone was eating, when the chat got on to depression, of all things.

"It's brain chemistry," I said. I'd reviewed a book on the topic for *The Trumpet.* It was a question of lacking a chemical—serotonin, a neurotransmitter which affected emotional states.

Heiner looked at me. "Life ees a challenge."

I agreed.

"You can't geeve up on life."

"No, you can't."

His eyes bored into me. "Then why *hafe* you?"

I was taken aback. "Eh, what?"

"Why geeven up?"

"I haven't."

He shook his head. "So young a voman cannot geeve up."

"Yes . . . I mean, no!"

Peter coughed and changed the subject.

We moved on to dessert—delicious raspberry-pink springy stuff. As the older girls served Heiner, I wondered what it would be like to have a father. Any kind of a father. Although mine would probably disapprove of me now, my memories of him were happy. He had smoked a pipe and smelt of tobacco like Peter. I remember him kissing me and tickling me. Then being so proud of me for winning a school prize for art. Maybe I had been his favourite, because he always called me "the queen". Then I had been the one who found him dead. I went to call him for dinner, but he was sitting in a chair, staring vacantly into space. When I couldn't rouse him, my mother had come in and quickly put me out of the room. Her tears were a terrible memory. Then a cousin had called round and taken my brother and me to her house. We went to the funeral, but that memory was a blur, and so was my father's face. Life went on because it had to. My mother missed him, yet always said she had had compensations in her children. She wasn't happy about my non-career, but William becoming a solicitor was the proudest thing in her life.

The Germans were early-bedders, so the evening ended around nine. We caught the bus home, and as it raced back in the dark, I quizzed Peter about Heiner's family.

He sighed happily. "Intelligent girls."

I agreed. "Good-looking, too."

"Heiner wants me to marry one of them."

I was shocked. "Oh . . . what about me?"

"I'm joking. If I *were* to leave the order, which I'm not."

"Wouldn't I be in the running?"

"It's your cultural background," he said matter-of-factly.

"I have a degree."

Peter shook his head. "You never get beyond the empirical."

"What's that?"

"It's the obvious—what's given. We're not intellectual equals. I'd have to marry someone compatible."

I was stunned by this but too hurt to say anything. Heiner's older daughters were probably still virgins, the state most valued by the Catholic Church. But Peter sounded like Nigel too. Wasn't I good enough for him? It had to be my mother's craving for grapes. He had called me beautiful on the bus: passionate, spiritual. Did he think I was inferior because I knew nothing about theology? Why hadn't I studied harder in college? The trouble was I hadn't known *how* to study. I hadn't even gone to tutorials. I did attend one, which was to be significant, but I didn't know it then.

About halfway home, I asked, "Why did Heiner say *that* about depression?"

Peter frowned. "What did he say?"

"He kept telling me to cheer up."

"He was sorry for you."

"Why?"

"I told him you were messing around with drugs."

I couldn't take it in at first. "You said I took aspirin?"

"No. Heroin."

"What?"

"I said you were shooting-up in the loo."

A vision of me shooting a gun came into my head.

"That's why you came upstairs after me?"

"I said I had to check up on you."

I didn't know what to say.

"Otherwise, he'd think it funny that I was with you. I said I couldn't leave you alone."

I swallowed. That's why the family hadn't been surprised to see us coming down together.

Peter didn't look penitent.

"That's it then," I said.

"What's it?"

"It's the end of our relationship."

He looked surprised. "Why?"

"Because I'm only for sex. I'm not good enough to marry."

"Louise . . ."

"You tell everyone lies about me!"

Peter was shocked into silence. He tried to talk to me again, accusing me of being humourless, but I wouldn't answer. After we got off the bus, I escaped from him, running down Serpentine Avenue. He followed, but couldn't catch me. It didn't look right to see a priest running.

Nine

"IT WAS A joke, Louise," he said outside the flat. "Open the door."

At first I refused, but in the end I did, as Declan came home. Peter apologised and said of course he would marry me if he could. He loved me and would do anything in the world for me. He hadn't meant to say that about the daughters. It had been Heiner's loopy idea for Peter to marry one of them. But that was *if* he left the order, which he wasn't planning to do. But one thing: *if we ever did get married,* I'd have to improve my bad language. He got into the habit of saying things like that: *"If we were married."* I saw it as a crack of light and I hoped he would one day leave the order for me. After our reconciliation that day, we made love again. It was difficult to refuse Peter—impossible. And so began my career as a drug addict. I was to be described as other things to Peter's friends: a manic depressive, a failed suicide, an ex-prisoner on parole, and an abused girlfriend—someone else's, of course.

How else could he explain me? Monks took vows of chastity.

Love needs a context, like humans need oxygen. And there was none for us. How could there be in the Ireland of the time? It was the last quarter of the twentieth century, and although de Valera had died the previous year, the country was still conservative. The year before, during the Theatre Festival, there had been walkouts from Tom Murphy's *The Sanctuary Lamp* because of the play's anti-clerical language. The Catholic Church had hardly changed at all. If anything, it had gone backwards, because some priests were allowed to marry in ancient times. The only progress: they now said mass facing the people so you could see what was going on. And it was in English and not Latin, so they didn't say *"Introibo ad altare dei."* Otherwise, we were still in the Dark Ages. People had the same extraordinary beliefs: we are not going to die and God cares.

It was now mid-February and I was home for Sunday lunch—I had missed three weeks running, so my mother was suspicious. She knew something was up, but I had been afraid to tell her the truth.

"You have a new boyfriend?"

"No." I was still determined to keep quiet about Peter. He wasn't actually a "boyfriend", so I didn't feel too dishonest now.

She looked disappointed.

My brother was also unmarried. Although he was her pride and joy, my mother loved me, I know. She claimed my not having been breastfed disproved the bonding theory, because she wasn't *close* to my brother, whom she had nursed for a whole year in her early marriage. Even though he had nibbled her to death, you couldn't have girl-talk with a son, she claimed. I didn't know about her bonding theory. I certainly lacked something. Was that why I had fallen so badly for Peter?

I pushed away my plate.

"Now what's the matter?"

"Nothing."

"It's unlike you to have a poor appetite, Louise."

She felt my forehead for a fever.

"You could have chronic fatigue syndrome."

"What's that?"

"Young people get it."

I sighed. "Oh . . . it's not that, Mum."

Something about her sympathy made me crack. "I'm in love."

"Now, that's good news!"

Kindness works better than torture. It's a wonder the tyrants haven't discovered that.

"Who is it?"

I couldn't answer.

She frowned. "Someone unsuitable?"

"Yes."

"Oh, dear. A married man?"

I said nothing.

"Louise, I don't—"

"It's a *priest.*"

"Well now!"

"There's no hope."

She looked intrigued, not shocked at all, but then my mother wasn't your typical mass-trotter. She was a serial romantic, and for years had visited my brother's school for hand-holding sessions with the Brothers, under the pretence of discussing his grades. When William was in the junior school, it had been one crush; then, as he had moved up the school, she had also progressed to senior masters. Young as I had been, I was glad she had something to look forward to, something besides those boring people in the Hospital Sweepstakes. That was full of frustrated widows. It was a grey place which reflected the grey Ireland of the day.

"I was afraid to tell you," I said.

She put her arms around me. "Oh, my poor darling."

I got weepy. "It's been a terrible time."

"He's ordained?"

I nodded.

"Then I assume he's getting laicised?"

I shook my head. "I don't think so."

Her eyes widened. "He must be."

"No."

She made a face. "He's *not* going to marry you?"

I shook my head. "Definitely not."

She frowned. "Hasn't Vatican II changed anything?"

"I don't think so."

The obsession with marriage was tiring. But again the thought of a future without Peter brought a lump to my throat and a funny tightness to my heart.

My mother was practical. "He should go on a retreat then."

"What good would that do?"

"It'd help him make up his mind."

"He's already made up his mind."

"Then he should leave you alone."

"He tries, then I come home from work and he's there, waiting."

I told her that our resolutions were hopeless. We were doomed lovers.

"I think you should talk to the Canon."

Nowadays we are sent to therapists for problems, but then you went to the priest. Canon FitzSimon had been our parish priest when my father had had his heart attack. Afterwards he had befriended my mother. He came to tea about twice a year and we had special blue china cups for the occasion. I had always thought that he was too old for her hit list; that he advised her about all sorts of practical things because she was a woman on her own. He had got my brother into a top solicitor's office, for instance, after he qualified, by twisting the arm of some other relative. Things were done like that in the Ireland of the day.

"Will I make an appointment for you?" she persisted.

"You can't tell *him*."

"I won't."

"Promise?"

"I promise."

But her promises meant nothing. My mother liked drama, and this was too good to keep. Our home was a telephone exchange: she phoned people all the time—about the weather, what to wear or eat. Whether Ireland should have joined the European Economic Community. Where were the best bargains in the sales? Who *I* was going out with. Who *William* was going out with. Or *not* going out with. So the Canon was the first to hear about Peter. Naturally he asked to see me.

I refused.

I knew what to expect. Apart from befriending my mother, there was nothing modern about him. He was a conservative of the old school. He had been decorated for bravery in the Spanish Civil War, but by the *wrong* side as far as I was concerned. He had supported Franco, which my mother didn't seem to notice. I had reminded her about the fascist atrocities, but she had shrugged, saying, "He has a medal for bravery," not realising it was awarded by a dictator. It shocked me at first, but I liked the Canon, even if he believed in rosaries and the stations of the cross. One good thing: he had never favoured the policies or statements of the late Archbishop of Dublin, John Charles McQuaid, who had confirmed me and whose stern portrait had stared down from the corridor wall in school. To me he had jelled with Pope Pius XII, and de Valera, so that I imagined all religious people must be thin with glasses. The Canon was different: he didn't wear glasses and he had a red, drinker's face. He was a member of the "loyal opposition", Tim had once told me. Being a journalist, he knew all about the ins, outs and wherefores of the Holy Irish Catholic Church.

The Canon kept asking to see me. He even sent messages via my mother. In the end he wrote to me.

Dear Louise,

It's been a long time since we had a chat. Could you phone me any afternoon after three for an appointment? I would like to see you.

Yours sincerely,

M. J. FitzSimon

I still refused, knowing he'd be outraged.

My mother was penitent. "No, he was very cross with *me.*"

"With *you?*"

"He accused me of betraying a confidence."

"Well, you did!"

She looked away. "I was worried, darling."

I had never learnt from my previous mistakes of confiding in her. I suppose other daughters would be angry, but my mother had had a disappointing life up to this. My news had been too hot to keep. It wasn't as good as having my engagement announced in *The Irish Times,* but it livened things up. God knows whom she had told at work, over lunch or at the coffee break. That thought made me queasy, and I imagined people whispering about me in the street.

I tried to be understanding. "I know you can't help it."

My mother hugged me. "What?"

"Being indiscreet."

"I just want your happiness, darling."

That was an impossibility, since meeting Peter, but to please her, I agreed to see the Canon.

Ten

HE LIVED IN the grey parochial house beside his church, which served a big south Dublin parish. The appointment was for three o'clock and I was on time. His bearded housekeeper opened the hall door and showed me to a spotless reception room. The furniture was big and uncomfortable, and there were hardbacks in an ugly mahogany bookcase. The smell of wax reminded me of the confessional.

I had been there before: when I was thirteen my mother had sent me for counselling. It was after an incident with the family doctor. I had visited the surgery for my sprained finger after playing netball, and he had touched my breast, getting all trembly. Then he examined my private parts. I said no, it was my *finger,* yet he had made me lie on a table and given me a full pelvic examination. Without knowing it, I had become an Irish cliché—a victim. When I confided in my mother, she got hysterical. Then a nurse told her I had been raped. But the Canon said that if no one else was present, it was probably just irregular. My mother went on and on about it. She told everyone, even my brother, who being practical had advised me to write to the doctor, demanding £5,000 to keep quiet and use it for a trip around the world. But it hadn't affected me at all. If I didn't know I had been abused, how could I have been? Unless it was the reason I had been so shocked by *The Ginger Man,* and couldn't enjoy sex with Nigel, but I didn't think so. Still, it might have made me over-religious: as a teenager, I had taken up fasting. I imagined myself as some saint and wanted to be canonized.

The Canon had said fasting for minors was against the teaching of the Church. He didn't believe in it. But that's how idiotic I was then. So I suppose it was wrong to say I wasn't ever religious. I just wasn't any more. Peter had said that prayer was "words into silence", and that was certainly true, because there was never any answer.

The Canon came in. His face was redder and his pitted Cyrano nose bigger.

"Louise, my dear child." As always, he hugged me.

After all, I'd known him since childhood. Some people didn't like priests, but the Canon had always been fatherly to my brother and me. He had given us holy pictures at our first communions and confirmations. When I was twelve, he had given me books on sex, which were confusing. One had said the man put his thing into a woman. I wondered if the Queen of England allowed that? There had been no sex education in school, and my mother always said I was too young to learn about it.

The Canon took a chair opposite me, his black soutane sweeping the floor as he sat down.

At first he chatted about the weather.

"Mum told you everything?" I blurted, wanting it over with.

"Yes. . . . My poor child." He shook his head.

There was concern in his voice, so I didn't know what to say. Next I was in tears: again I had cracked from kindness.

The Canon offered me a folded hanky. "Now, now, stop this."

"Thanks," I managed to say, taking a deep breath. "I'm in love and there's no hope."

He didn't seem put out by my news, although you couldn't tell from his red face.

"I have to compete with God."

"I know."

"It isn't fair."

"Life isn't fair. We don't always get what we want."

I started crying again.

He stood up and went to the door. "Would you like a cup of tea?"

I nodded, managing to control myself.

He disappeared, but came back after a few minutes. His dreary housekeeper followed, rattling a tray of teacups, a teapot and slices of fruitcake. She set it down, giving me a suspicious look. I vowed that if I ever grew a beard, I would have it surgically removed.

The Canon dismissed her. "Thank you, Mrs Kelly."

"Will I not pour, Canon?" she asked.

"No, it's all right."

She left, glaring at me.

As soon as the door was shut, I started crying again.

"Now, Louise, you'll have to pull yourself together."

I took a breath.

"And this young man will have to stop upsetting you."

"He's not young."

He frowned. "What age is he?"

"Thirty-three. The age of Jesus Christ."

"Old enough to know better."

"We've tried to give each other up."

The Canon got annoyed. "You'll just have to try harder."

"He blames me for everything."

"He's not a man then."

I thought about this. "He feels guilty."

"It's cowardly to blame you."

"I suppose you'll tell on him?"

"Who on earth would I tell?"

"I dunno. The bishop. His order."

"I don't betray confidences."

"My mother tells everyone."

He was annoyed again. "She shouldn't do that."

I wiped my eyes. "She told you. And God knows who else."

He poured the tea, passing me a cup. "Don't worry. I'll stop her."

"You'll have to disconnect the phone."

He laughed. "I can't do that, but I'll talk to her." He looked away, changing the subject. "Drink your tea. Have some cake. Things aren't always as bad as they seem."

I took a bite of the cake. It was stale, but I ate it anyway, looking around the uncomfortable room. It was a lonely life with only a housekeeper for company. "Don't you want some?"

He shook his head. "I know what you're going through, my dear."

My mouth was full. How could he know about love?

"Remember, love is God's gift."

"Even loving a priest?"

He gave me a sad look. "In a way, yes."

"I thought it was forbidden."

"All love comes from God."

I knew then what I had always suspected: the Canon was one of my mother's conquests. He was speaking from experience. All those afternoon teas had been a cover-up. I remember once noticing how he looked at her: his eyes had that "candle in the darkness" look. It was in a hospital room and my mother had had a hysterectomy. She had said something irreverent and he had laughed. I had always wanted someone to look at me like that. The Canon must have loved my mother for all those years. He was a good guy. *"Thou art FitzSimon, and upon this rock, I will build my church."* Jesus hadn't said anything about celibacy being a requirement. The Canon would have made a good husband. He could have been our stepfather. If he had been, my brother might have had someone to play chess with and I mightn't have turned out a mess. The thought of my miseries made me break down again.

"Now, Louise, stop that!"

"OK." I dabbed my eyes.

The Canon must have read my mind. "A priest takes vows of celibacy to be available to everyone. If he was married, his wife would have to come first."

"I thought God hated sex."

He shook his head. "God gave us the gift of sex."

"It's a gift?"

"A gift not to be abused. That young man is abusing you."

The Canon didn't blame me: if anyone was doing wrong, it was Peter. That made a change.

He suggested I keep in touch. Meantime, I was to go places and cheer myself up. I said a play by Beckett was on at the Focus.

He frowned. "You like him?"

I nodded. "He's brilliant."

"He preaches a philosophy of despair."

"I love his plays."

He advised me to find something less depressing.

On the way out, I studied his books. Everything was there: philosophy, biographies and some Victorian novels.

"Why don't you borrow one?" he asked.

I wondered if he had anything about Héloïse and Abelard.

He found a biography of Abelard. "You're not the first to love a priest."

"Ours is a parallel story." I didn't want to mention that even the names were the same: Louise and Peter.

He flicked through the book. "Abelard was the founder of Nominalism."

"What's that?"

He thought for a second. "He rejected universals in philosophy. There are no realities other than the concrete."

"I see," I said, but I didn't really.

He handed me the book. "In some ways the twelfth century was more liberal than ours."

"Castration wasn't very liberal?"

He swallowed. "No, but that wasn't the Church. It was Héloïse's family."

"Did Abelard marry anyone else?"

"No. Remember, your situation is not new. The Church has always had problems with celibacy."

In the hall I said, "I don't know what's going to happen."

"Only one thing *can* happen."

I didn't want to hear it.

"You must pray for strength."

"To give him up?"

He nodded, shaking my hand.

I had no strength where Peter was concerned.

Eleven

DESPITE THE CANON'S advice, our affair went on. We were two people on a raft-ride to destruction. Neither of us had the sense to jump before the white water. I began the Canon's book to discover that Héloïse hadn't regretted her love for Abelard; not one bit. Well, neither did I. Peter was the best thing in my life. No matter how painfully, I was alive.

It was still the same: sex followed by Peter's good resolutions. But I needn't have worried, because he always came back. By now I was in the habit of hiding my key under a stone in the garden, so Peter was usually inside when I returned from work, as if it were the most normal thing in the world. And, of course, the best or the worst happened, depending on your viewpoint.

Things at the Claremont were getting bad. Amanda had never liked me. One night Brigid took me for a drink, explaining that the manageress was the same to everyone. She had picked on Brigid, too, when she had worked there. It still upset me. I suppose I wanted to be liked, even by Amanda. In rare good moods, she'd tell me about her other *hawf,* always in a boastful way. He was a chef and they went sailing in Dun Laoghaire. They were planning to open a restaurant and were saving for a house, too. It sounded great and a far cry from anything on my horizon.

"Do you have another *hawf?"* she asked.

"I broke up with my boyfriend." I meant Nigel. Telling her about Peter would be too complicated.

One day Peter appeared at the end of lunch hour.

I went over. "What is it?"

He threw down his duffle bag. "Nothing. I had to see you."

I looked round. What if someone recognised him? Did he have something in mind?

"You shouldn't come here," I whispered.

"It's a public house, Louise."

"Someone might see you."

He was irked. "I'm hungry. I want some lunch."

I showed him the menu. "The steak's good."

He snapped the menu shut. "I'll have that. And plenty of chips."

Peter ate his lunch with his eyes on me. If I served anyone and joked or laughed with them, he got agitated. As I was giving him the bill, he asked, "What time will you be home?"

"Brigid and I are going to the pictures." The latest Bergman film was on in town.

He looked disappointed. "I'll come about eight."

"We may not be back by then."

"I'll wait."

"OK, my key will be under the stone."

He put on his coat and left.

Afterwards Amanda was curious. She flicked back her bandana. "Who on earth was that?"

"A friend."

"He looked like *more."*

"What do you mean?"

"He seemed keen on you."

"He's just a friend," I lied.

"He's awfully good-looking. Where did you meet him?"

"Trinity."

"Trinity? You studied there?"

"I didn't. It was at a party."

"You go to parties there?"

I nodded, wanting her to shut up. I had never been to a party in Trinity, because niggardly Nigel had never invited me. Once he'd asked me to an English Department seminar and everyone had stared. They were discussing T. S. Eliot, but it was for staff members only. It was most uncomfortable: I didn't know whether to leave or stay. It had cured me of all interest in the college. But I shouldn't have said what I did to Amanda, because she hated me even more from then on.

After closing for the holy hour, we were served lunch by the chef—whatever was left over. It was a good lunch and it saved money. One day I had mine on a tray and carried it across the pub to where Amanda was sitting with one of the owners. He got up to leave as I approached their table—up to this we had always sat together with other staff, so it wasn't anything unusual. But, as I put down my tray, Amanda said, "You're not allowed here."

"I'm not?"

"Stawff are at the *other* table."

"Oh." Then I noticed the kitchen and waiting staff at a table on the far side of the pub.

"This is for management," she said.

"Management?"

"You're *not* management."

"No. Sorry."

It upset me, although I didn't want to sit with her. It was just what I had always done. The next day, in the middle of a busy lunch hour, she pounced on me again.

"You're too slow, Louise."

"What do you mean?"

"I mean, slow. S-l-o-w."

"Oh."

"You'll have to hurry up!"

"I'm going as fast as I can."

"Clear those tables by the bar and take the orders here."

I cleared the tables, carrying a full tray over to the washing-up hatch. About halfway across, I tripped over a loose carpet. There was a horrible crash.

Conversation stopped: everyone stared.

Amanda ran over. "Clean up that mess! Get a dustpan and brush!"

I picked up the pieces. "Sorry."

"This will be deducted from your wages, Louise."

"It was an accident."

Red-faced, she scraped some mashed potato and turnip into a napkin. "You'll be hearing more about this."

The next Friday, when I collected my wages from the head office in town, there was a note in my envelope, saying five pounds had been docked for breakages.

I couldn't stand Amanda's bullying behaviour, so I answered an ad in the evening paper.

OFFICE ASSISTANT WANTED

Assistant to advertising manager needed for busy northside magazine office. Must have good typing speeds and decent shorthand. Apply in writing.

It was a proper job.

My typing was fifteen words a minute, but I had no shorthand. Still, I had worked in a magazine before, so I knew it was only a matter of sending out invoices and seeing to subscriptions. There had been a lot of sitting around in my last job, in between avoiding the editor's tantrums. He was fond of throwing coffee cups, while screaming about some minor mistake, so anything would be an improvement.

The northside would get me away from Sandymount and was two bus journeys from Peter's monastery. Deep down, I knew we couldn't go on indefinitely, and this would be a different world and a distraction. You practically needed a visa to cross the Liffey—more so than today. Everything looked drabber there. The people seemed smaller and undernourished. It was greyer and rainier. Maybe that was me, but I don't know where those feelings came from.

The magazine promoted the antique furniture trade; it consisted of freelance articles by experts, photographs and ads—which paid production costs. There were two other staff: Shane Cassidy, the advertising manager, and Miss Walsh, the office manager. Shane, who was in his late forties, was hardly ever in the office; he spent his time walking around Dublin, soliciting ads from antique shops. He worked on commission and had some special arrangement with the editor for expenses.

"Take a seat," Shane said at my interview.

I sat on the edge of a chair.

He put his feet on the desk, while he glanced at my CV. He was Irish-looking, with long, greying hair, thick sideburns and a small compact body.

He spoke with a thick Dublin accent. "Ye have office experience?"

I nodded, looking nervously at the other interviewer, who said nothing.

Miss Walsh was also middle-aged with long red nails, red lips and a bouffant hairstyle like an elderly Jackie Kennedy. She wore a suit, with a matching frilly blouse, and walked with a forward-tilting gait, like someone on stilts.

I felt her disapproval from the start. Was she going to be another Amanda? She stared at my chest, so I resolved to look for a bra that would flatten me. I envied small-breasted women and wanted to be thirty or thirty-one inches or, better still, to have no breasts at all. Mine had only got me into trouble with Peter.

Miss Walsh pursed her lips. “You're willing to take a speed test?”

I hesitated, knowing I'd fail.

Before I could say anything, Shane dismissed her. “Sure, any eejit can type!”

This brought more pursed lips. “I disagree,” she said.

Shane asked where I had worked last.

“I'm a freelance journalist . . . eh, hoping to be full-time.”

He looked impressed. “You write for the newspapers?”

I nodded. I didn't want to mention *The Catholic Trumpet.* “There's good money in it—except people are slow to pay.”

“Why don't ye sue 'em?”

“I'm only a freelancer.”

He lit up. “So yer able to work on yer own?”

I assured him I was.

He looked at Miss Walsh. “We need someone who can work on their own.”

Although she didn't look happy, I got the job. Maybe my luck was changing.

The magazine's editor lived in Belfast and was a “mean bollocks”, according to Shane, who was the best thing about my new job. His real name was Seán, but he had changed it after seeing the famous movie *Shane* as a child. He was an actor and part-time conceptual artist. Neither occupation paid much, so he needed the income from selling the ads. He was a sort of latter-day Leopold Bloom. A true Dub, originally from the inner city—Sheriff Street, I think—he had gone to Germany as a teenager, where he had won a scholarship to a famous gymnastic academy. Later he had toured the world with a company of acrobats, and then had retired back to Ireland at the age of forty because of knee injuries from all that leaping around. He regularly got parts in small theatres around Dublin and had shows in galleries where he lay in a coffin, pretending to be dead. This was conceptual art: but I learnt these things later.

Shane did everything to make me feel welcome. On my second day, he put a small white package on my desk.

"What is it?"

It looked like dried herbs wrapped in grease-proof paper.

He put a finger to his lips, rolling his eyes at Miss Walsh's back.

I hid it in my handbag.

He grew the marijuana in his hot-press and from then on gave me a weekly packet. He brought it into the office, the way people brought duty-free whiskey back from a holiday. I didn't smoke, but didn't have the nerve to tell him, so I saved it in an old tea tin at the flat. I didn't know what else to do with it. One day I decided I was missing something and came back from work, planning to try a joint. I had bought rolling tobacco along with cigarette papers in the newsagent's. It would relax me, if I could manage to inhale without getting sick.

The tea tin was empty.

Someone had stolen the marijuana!

It had to be Declan. He was a thief as well as a sadist.

If I had been a drug addict, it would have been shitty, but I didn't care. Brigid was furious, although she disapproved of pot and never smoked it either.

"I was wondering what it was," she said. "I thought it was parsley and you were going in for cooking."

"Sorry. I should have told you."

"We could've been raided by the guards."

"Sorry."

"That's it. Declan's going!"

I hesitated. "We need his rent money. You're leaving in a few weeks."

"You'll get someone else."

"It's mid-term now. Everyone will be fixed up."

We confronted Declan that night. Besides the loud music, his untidiness was driving us crazy. He never cleaned the kitchen and always left the bathroom in a disgusting state. Stealing the pot was too much.

Brigid had her teacher expression on. "Did you steal Louise's marijuana?"

He looked blank. "What marijuana?"

"The marijuana in the tea tin."

"What are youse talking about?"

Brigid was firm. "You know right well! You stole it, didn't you?"

"I didn't, man, I swear."

"I'm not a man!" She pointed to me. "Do we look like men?"

He put his hand mockingly across his breast. "Sorry, no, youse don't."

He went to his room.

Brigid followed him. "What about the pot?"

"Musta been that guy Peter."

This lie got to me. "We know you're lying, Declan! Peter doesn't smoke pot."

As he turned his back, Brigid called after him, "Since you don't have the decency to apologise, you can leave!"

He turned. "Youse are throwing me out?"

"Yes," I joined in nervously. "I couldn't live with a thief."

"I have me rights. Youse are rack-renters!"

Brigid was furious. "How dare you say that?"

"Youse are makin' me pay double!"

How had he found out? It wasn't double, he was paying half the rent and there were three of us. But Brigid had a tiny room, almost a cupboard.

"You have the biggest room!" she shouted. "And you owe this month's rent."

"I'm not payin! Youse owe me!"

"Find another flat!"

Declan did the Nazi salute and slammed his door.

She shouted that we'd call the guards. Of course, we couldn't in the circumstances. In the end we didn't have to, because he left in the middle of the night, owing us the rent. But it was OK: we had his deposit.

Twelve

I PUT ANOTHER ad under the Trinity arches. This time I deleted *Smokers Welcome,* but there had been no replies by Brigid's departure day.

I felt lonely. We had had great times: shopping in the Dandelion Market on Saturdays where we had once bought matching velvet maxi skirts made of old curtains. On these expeditions, we always had lunch in town. In the evenings we walked on Sandymount Strand and went to the pub afterwards. She had advised me about Miss Walsh's hostility, too, saying it was jealousy and to ignore her. Brigid said that some women like only men; they hate other women. It was hard to understand. Why would anyone be jealous of me? I don't think I had ever been jealous. Oh, maybe I envied the way things had worked out for Brigid. She had met Sam in Barry's Hotel off Parnell Square, after an All-Ireland semi-final, and the next thing they were getting married. He had a cottage in Kerry and they were going into organic farming. Carrots were the one vegetable that have to be organic because of being *in* the earth, she had told me. Organic carrots were unheard of then—everyone ate ordinary carrots—but Brigid and Sam were ahead of their time. The wedding was to be in the autumn. I was invited, not to be bridesmaid, but as a special guest.

Brigid was in her bedroom, packing clothes into a suitcase and books into boxes for later collection by Sam.

"What do you think of these trousers?" I asked from the door.

She looked up. "They're too tight."

They were the latest bell bottoms. I pulled the brown clingy material away from my crotch.

"Oh hell, they cost a fortune."

"How much?"

I was afraid to say. "They were on sale in Pia Bangs."

"Trying to impress your man?"

"No, I have to look smart for my job."

"You never bothered before."

Your man was Brigid's name for Peter. She disapproved more and more, but I felt this was judgemental because she didn't know him well. They had met a few more times, when she had come back to the flat unexpectedly and he had been in the sitting room having a coffee after one of our sessions.

"He's using you." She squeezed the case shut.

I helped her carry it to the hall.

"He shouldn't come here."

"He can't help it."

She shrugged. "Well . . ."

"I told you: we're in love."

"Listen, I asked before and I'll ask again: what's he offering?"

"Nothing, I suppose."

"That's just it."

"He can't *offer* anything. He's not allowed."

"Then forget him."

"I can't."

Brigid looked sympathetic for a change. "Love isn't a bolt from heaven. It's a contract between two people."

I didn't see it like that. I had tried to separate myself from Peter, but couldn't. I counted the hours and the minutes between his visits to the flat.

"You have a contract with Sam?" I asked.

"Not yet, but it's not all one-sided."

Our affair wasn't either. Peter had risked damnation for me. His immortal soul could be lost for breaking his vows, which he did out of love. He believed in Jesus and hell and all that, so it was worse for him than for me. It had to be.

Brigid broke the silence. "I don't want you hurt."

"I've never experienced love before."

She sighed. "You've got it bad."

"I know."

"I *hate* leaving you with him."

"There's no need to worry."

"I do worry. You're my best friend. What'll happen if you get pregnant?"

"Peter's an expert."

"At what?"

"Pulling out."

She hooted with laughter. "If in doubt, pull out. That doesn't work."

"It has so far."

"I can't believe he's not using contraceptives. Sperm can live for weeks."

"But it's not getting *in* me."

Brigid was unconvinced. In the end we agreed to disagree. When she was packed, we had a last cup of tea in the kitchen.

"I'll miss you," I said.

"I think you should go back to living at home."

I was shocked.

"Give up the flat. It'll get you away from your man."

"I can't go home."

"How'll you pay the rent here?"

"I'll find someone."

"I wish you'd never met Peter."

"He's not that bad."

"He is. He's bad news."

As I said: Brigid was black and white and had never heard of grey.

I helped her with her cases to Busáras. The station was smoky and crowded and I got a sudden urge to jump on a bus and go somewhere too. I'd manage with a few things in a handbag: a toothbrush, change of underwear, one spare blouse. I could forget Peter, my whole previous life.

We joined the queue for Kerry, pushing her luggage into the hold of the parked bus.

She kissed me tearfully. "Promise to visit me."

"I will."

"But don't bring your man!"

You didn't argue with Brigid. She disliked Peter and always would, no matter what he said or did. I waved her off, feeling lonely as the bus pulled into the afternoon traffic for the long journey south. Then I walked all the way back to Sandymount where I put on my one Bob Dylan LP. All evening he screeched at me to go away from his window, leave at my own chosen speed. He wasn't the one I wanted, he wasn't the one I needed. Was it a message?

I got more and more depressed. Bob Dylan was proof of how far you could go with a scratchy voice. But would the lyrics be prophetic? I went to bed thinking of what Brigid had said about love being a contract. Could feelings be measured in such terms?

Thirteen

I WAS NOW without a flatmate. No one answered my Trinity notice, so I tried the *Evening Herald* under flats to let.

WANTED

Person to share beautiful basement flat with one other. Own bedroom. Sea views. All mod cons. Non-smoker preferred. Phone 695662 any evening.

The ad ran for four nights—for the price of three. You phoned in the words and the paper sent on the bill, which, when it came, was easy to ignore. You could have moved flats by the time they threatened "to take steps". And they probably wouldn't bother for such a pittance. That was my thinking at the time. It was immature, but I convinced myself that necessity knows no law.

I called upstairs to pay the landlady.

Miss P. Pym was somewhere between fifty and seventy. I couldn't tell anyone's age then. I'm still bad about age. I can see children are young and babies are babies, but grown-ups were and are a puzzle to me. Miss Pym seemed older because of her grey hair, but she could have been middle-aged. We didn't know her Christian name. It was probably Primrose or Priscilla—Patricia would have been too ordinary. She was a spinsterish type, who wore twin sets and pearls and had an older Scottish boyfriend, Gordon, who could have been in his seventies. He was on a permanent visit. At least I assumed he was visiting, because I couldn't imagine anything else. Not with people their age.

I was nervous of her saying something about Declan's wild party, but she was friendly and invited me into her antique-filled double front room. It was like stepping backwards into Miss Pym's childhood. Everything was so elegant. The standard lamp had a fringed shade, the chairs were covered in flowery pink loose covers, and the mahogany sideboard was covered with heavy silver. I could tell that nothing had changed here since her parents' time.

Her cat jumped on me. It was an expensive breed, with long, allergenic hair and sharp claws, which dug into my lap as I pushed it off. I couldn't help not being a cat lover, although Miss Pym didn't seem to notice.

When I told her about Brigid having gone, her eyebrows arched in dismay.

"You mean she's *left?*"

Brigid's reliability had impressed her.

"She'll be back . . . for a visit."

Miss Pym was frowning. "She co-signed the lease. She could have said something."

Teachers were considered trustworthy, more than freelancers doubling as waitresses.

"And what happened to that strange creature in the sunglasses?"

"Declan's gone too."

"That's just as well. I'm sure you miss Nigel."

I said nothing. Nigel had been a disgusting suck-up.

"He was such a nice young man. Well, I'll have to draw up another lease."

I said it wasn't necessary.

She got cross. "I can't have every Tom, Dick and Harry here."

"No." Then I got up my courage. "Would you reduce the rent?"

"I'm afraid not, Louise. I know you're on your own, but I could rent that flat in the morning."

Although it was a dive without any central heating, the address was good, and in those days, renters queued around corners as soon as flats were advertised. It was hard to find somewhere to live, so I didn't anticipate moving and agreed to go on paying on my own until I found someone to share. Before leaving, I got the usual lecture about drawing the curtains.

My *Herald* ad appeared to have been a waste, but I hadn't spent good money on it. Now I would have no scruple in returning the invoice: *not known at this address.*

Then Felicity turned up: the friend who started me on this story by nudging me to email Peter in Canada. Felicity was one of those born aristocrats. It was an aristocracy of spirit. Although rich and from a legal background—her father was a famous judge—she was unspoilt. Exceptionally thin because of some delicacy in childhood, she was my age, but her clothes made her look older. She often wore a tailored, black, pin-striped suit; and she was wearing one that day. A woman stockbroker, she had an aura of money. It was a world I knew nothing about.

"Hi, I'm Louise."

We shook hands.

"Felicity Moore."

Her gold watch matched rings and a bracelet; her shoulder bag was soft leather. I guessed she would have no trouble with the rent, so I tried to impress her by mentioning that the sitting room, which I had cleaned scrupulously, got the sun all day.

"It does," she said, scanning the room with approval. "It's wonderful."

I stared at the floor. "The carpet needs replacing, I know."

"No, it's bohemian."

"Well, yes, but the couch is a bit threadbare."

"Oh, no, it's just right."

She walked around, admiring everything. From the bedroom, which was to be hers and from which I had vacuumed and scrubbed all traces of Declan, she peered out the window to the front garden.

"Where are the sea views?"

"From the top of the house."

She cleared her throat.

"The ad was a mistake," I explained. "It was meant to say "*proximity* to sea."

I hoped she wouldn't ask to see the other side of the horsehair mattress, which was the worse for someone's weak kidneys. Brigid and I had bought it second-hand in the Simon charity shop, but Felicity was too polite and trusting to ask me to turn it.

Instead she quizzed me, noticing the battered typewriter on the dining room table. "And what do you do?"

I told her I was a freelance journalist.

"How interesting."

"I work part-time as a typist too. To support my journalism."

"What paper do you write for?"

"The Catholic Trumpet."

"I don't know it."

"They sell it in some newsagents. And outside the church. It's a Catholic paper."

She looked disappointed. "I'm Church of Ireland."

"I'll get you a copy. I write for other papers too." It was only a white lie.

"I think I've seen your name."

"It's been in a few papers."

We were getting on well. Felicity did one more tour of the flat and seemed to be making private mental calculations.

Then she said, "My father can drive me on Saturday. Can I move in then?"

I hid my surprise. "Yes, yes, of course."

We agreed on a time for her to come with her stuff. Since she was so well-off, I didn't ask for a deposit, but she insisted on giving me one, plus a month's rent in advance.

Felicity's office hours were long and her evenings taken up by a barrister boyfriend, so I saw her only late at night, when we would chat over a cup of cocoa. She was musical and often commented on Peter's guitar, which he left in the flat. Sometimes, she would ask me about him, but I was always evasive, so she didn't press me. For some reason, I imagined she would be shocked by our relationship and deluded myself that she never guessed the truth. She must have met Peter when he came to the flat, but I couldn't remember any exact occasion. I felt older than her, not in years, but in experience. We didn't become close until later in life when she visited me in New York, and even then, I could never bring myself to tell her the truth. The irony was that she knew all the time. But discretion was one of Felicity's virtues: again it was something to do with her being Church of Ireland.

At the time, her presence in the flat was consoling, and because of her, I didn't miss Brigid quite so much. Peter and I were still treading water, unable to make any decision about the future. I suppose I hoped he would leave the order, but he still said nothing about it.

Meantime love had its drawbacks: we never did anything normal. It was frustrating not going to plays or the cinema, or even to the pub. I said this to Peter once.

"OK, we'll go to the movies," he said.

I couldn't believe it.

"I don't want you to have bad memories."

"So you're going to be a memory?"

"Some day I'll have to be, but today we're going to a movie."

We went to a thriller in the Academy—I forget what it was called. It was just like every other bang-bang and not my thing, but I loved being out with Peter and pretended to enjoy it. Afterwards we went to the Indian Tea Room, where we met a woman friend of his from the Canadian embassy and he got all flustered, neglecting to introduce me.

Afterwards, we ran into my mother in Grafton Street. She had come into town for a sale.

"Hello, Mum," I said, feeling my heart thump.

She gave Peter a knowing look.

"This is eh, Peter," I said, concealing his surname.

"Delighted to meet you, *Father,*" she said.

After some embarrassed small talk, we moved on in opposite directions. Peter was in shock. "How does she know I'm a priest?"

"I told her I *met* a priest; she's guessing it's you."

"You told her about us?"

"No, of course not!"

He was relieved and calmed down, but it was our only venture in to town. After that, we stayed in the flat, making *"one little room an everywhere"*. After sex, we always had dinner, then he played his classical guitar. Peter usually brought wine from the monastery in his duffle bag and sometimes bottles of their ancient Guinness. It was flat, but had an interesting rusty taste. He was generous, or the order was. I hoped they wouldn't miss it.

Fourteen

THE EVE OF St Patrick's Day, I was home writing another review for *The Trumpet* when Peter rang from the Ecumenical Centre.

"There's a party here. Why don't you come over?"

I could hear laughter down the line. Although delighted to be asked, I said I was busy. I must have been playing hard to get.

"Come on over. I want you to meet some people."

That was a change. "Who?"

"People who'll help with your journalism."

"I should get on with my review."

"Louise, I'm trying to help you. Now come on over."

Peter had said something about getting me interviews for *The Trumpet.* He had contacts in the Ecumenical Centre. It was a comfortable red-bricked family house in south Dublin, which had been converted into a centre for the reunification of Christianity. In the garden, spring flowers were already out and a cherry tree had begun to blossom. The house had a reception room, a library and study rooms in what had once been attic bedrooms.

A wine and cheese was in progress when I arrived.

Catholic priests, lay people and Protestant ministers were chatting.

There was a definite buzz. I could tell who the Protestant clerics were by the grey cardigans and collars. Sandra, the secretary, a middle-aged woman with short white hair and stern winged spectacles, passed around red and white wine.

I reached for red, but she pulled the tray away.

"Put that back!"

"What?"

"I'll get you orange juice."

"Oh . . . thanks," I said. "Eh—I'd prefer wine."

"You're not to drink. Put it back!"

I was shocked, but obeyed.

It was peculiar behaviour. I'd heard of Protestants being mean, but this was a bit much. Hadn't the changing of water into wine been Jesus's first miracle? Or did she think I was underage? Then it hit me: Peter was saving me again. He had told her I was an alcoholic.

Then I saw him across the hall in a group of people. He was wearing civvies—brown corduroy trousers and a black polo neck sweater—and was with another red-haired man. From the other man's conservative way of dressing, I had a hunch he was a priest too: the friend called Pat, who also loved a woman. What had Peter told him about me in confession?

Peter beckoned, so I made my way through the crowd.

Heiner and Johanna, his German friends, were there.

"You remember Heiner and Johanna," he said.

I said hello. How could I forget our visit?

"Ah, de girl who ees tired of life," Heiner joked. "How *are* you?"

"I'm fine."

"And this is Father Pat," Peter said.

As someone grabbed Peter's elbow, we shook hands. A freckled complexion matched the red hair. He was smiling. Peter couldn't have said anything bad about me.

"Hello, Father," I said.

"It's Pat. Forget the titles. You must be Louise?"

I nodded.

"You're living down in Sandymount, and you write for the *The Trumpet?*"

I nodded again, as Sandra came over with a glass of water. I took it from her without saying anything.

"She doesn't drink," she said to Pat.

He looked understanding. "That's wise."

Before I could say I did, Peter returned, winking at Pat. "We have to keep an eye on her."

I sipped the water, embarrassed.

We must have talked about something. It was so long ago, I don't remember the details: maybe my prospects in journalism. Then I was introduced to Andrew, one of the grey cardigans and the reason I had been invited. He had heard that I was an aspiring journalist and, on Peter's suggestion, had agreed to give me an interview about Irish ecumenism. I was to write an article about the Centre for *The Trumpet* and impress my editor. Maybe I could even do a series of articles: I'd be on my way. Because I was Peter's friend, everyone wanted to help, so I wrote down contact telephone numbers, arranging to ring Andrew for an appointment the next day.

This calmed my anger at Peter. An alcoholic wasn't as bad as being a manic depressive or a drug addict. I watched as Andrew kissed a woman goodbye. Why was it OK for Church of Ireland ministers to kiss women? Andrew probably had a wife, too, to whom he could make love. Why was it so wrong for Peter and me?

I didn't want to be seen leaving with Peter, so after several glasses of orange juice, I slipped away. I asked Sandra for the loo on the way out and was directed to the first landing.

Coming out, I bumped into Peter.

He grabbed my arm. "Where are you going?"

"Downstairs, then home."

"You can't go now."

"Why not?"

"I want you to meet more people."

He was breathing heavily, so I suspected the worst. Why did he get turned on in other people's houses? Before I could say anything, he bustled me up to the next landing.

"What are you doing?"

He opened one of the small attic bedrooms and backed me in, following and locking the door.

"Take off your clothes!"

I thought he was drunk.

"What?"

"You heard me!"

"We can't! Not here!"

He kissed me, the way he always did. The next minute he was undressing me and pulling me down on a couch covered with a tartan rug.

"Oh my God, you're wearing stockings!" he moaned, grabbing my thighs. "Are they for me?"

What was he talking about?

"How did you know I liked suspenders?"

"I didn't!"

"But you're wearing them."

"The stockings are for my allergy!" I whispered. It was too embarrassing to explain, even to someone as liberal as Peter, how tights irritated me.

"Walk over there!"

I started pulling on my clothes. Did he think I was some sort of striptease artist?

"What are you doing?"

"I'm going home! You're a pervert."

"Later . . . please!" He held my wrist. "I'll walk you home."

I pulled free. "Someone might come in."

For reply, he put a finger to my lips.

"Don't refuse me now."

The accusatory tone got to me: I suppose I didn't want to be a tease. I could see an erection bulging under his trousers. He took them off as I looked nervously at the risen member hidden by underpants. This time there was no foreplay. In a minute it was inside me and we were making love on the couch. The whole room seemed to vibrate. At first I worried about the noise, but then got carried away, too. As always, Peter had hit the "on" button.

Then someone knocked on the door. There was a pin-drop silence.

I was unable to breathe.

More loud knocking.

Peter called out, "Yes?"

"Peter, Andrew would like to talk to you about the next committee meeting." It was Sandra—she knew.

I was quaking, but Peter kept cool. "I'm counselling Miss O'Neill. You can say I'll be down in fifteen minutes."

She hesitated. "Right." Silence. Then through gritted teeth: "I'll tell him!"

I got my breath.

Peter held a finger to my lips, afraid to move.

"What am I this time?" I whispered, as her footsteps receded down the stairs. "Pregnant and going for an abortion?"

The fear of discovery had deflated everything.

He pulled out of me and began dressing. "Just behave yourself."

I started crying.

"I'm not an alcoholic."

"I know you're not."

"You told them I was."

"Who?"

"Downstairs."

"I didn't."

"Then why wouldn't Sandra give me any wine?"

"She's mean."

"You told her I'm a drunk."

He looked guilty. "Louise, try and understand. I had to explain what I was doing with you."

"Couldn't you tell the truth?"

"You know I can't." He held my shoulders and stared into my eyes. "I love you, Louise. You ought to know that by now."

If this was love, it was awful.

"You don't understand the 'reality of the situation'."

I understood it OK: hole-in-the-corner sex for the rest of my life.

We got dressed and went downstairs, ignoring the way people looked with embarrassment at the ground rather than at us. I don't know how they knew, but they did. I lingered awkwardly in the hall, waiting for Peter while he chatted to Andrew. Across the room, Sandra was in conversation with Father Pat. Her cheeks were red with irritation, and I felt myself wilt under her accusing gaze, which said: *I know what you've been up to! And it's always the woman's fault. Men don't have control over their passions. They are likely to explode if tempted by the likes of you.*

I had met her type before. A nun in school used to tell us not to go to the pictures alone. A man would come with ether on a hanky and press it to our faces, then drag us out to an alleyway, and there we would undergo a fate worse than death. It had never happened to me, but then I'd never been to the pictures on my own. What would the nuns think of me now?

Sandra kept staring: I stared back. It wasn't my fault. Why not blame Peter, who had dragged me upstairs and pushed me into a room? Damn her, I thought, and picked up someone's leftover red wine, drinking it down quickly. She had seen me, but I looked away. I had a fantasy of Jesus blessing it and saying, *"This is for you, Louise. It's not the best wine, but it's all I have."*

Father Pat was saying goodbye to a nearby group.

I moved away, so as not to appear to be listening.

He stopped beside me on his way out. "You aren't looking too happy, Louise."

"I'm fine."

"You are?"

Tears came.

He squeezed my arm, sighing. "Ah . . . I thought so."

I wiped my eyes with a sleeve. Did he know what had happened upstairs too? Did I have a mark on my forehead?

He looked across the room to Peter, who was chatting to Andrew. "Peter's a terrible man."

I said nothing.

"What's he done now?"

"He's told everyone I'm an alcoholic. I'm not."

"Sticks and stones will break my bones, but names will never hurt me." He shook his head again. "A terrible man."

"He's the most beautiful man I've ever met. That's the whole problem."

Pat didn't reply.

"He's just so cold," I said.

He looked puzzled. "Cold?"

"The whole Catholic Church is cold to women."

He patted my arm. "Peter's not the whole Church. Listen, he's going to be held up here. How about a drink?"

I had to laugh. "A drink?"

"That's what I said."

"Aren't you afraid I'll tear up the place?"

Pat squeezed my arm again. Before I could say more, he crossed the room and said something to Peter. Peter looked at his watch, then nodded. As Pat came back, he said, "We'll go to Horse Show House. Peter's joining us later."

The pub was on my way home. It was full of rugby types with girls fawning around them. I envied their uncomplicated lives and felt lonely for Nigel and his Mini. It hadn't been such a bad relationship. If only I hadn't been so uptight about marriage, maybe I could have co-operated, but you don't know yourself until it's too late.

Pat found a seat in the corner. "What are you having?"

I ordered a lager and lime.

He went to the bar and came back with two glasses.

I groped in my bag. "I have money."

He laughed. "I don't allow women to pay."

"What about your vow of poverty?"

"I still don't allow it."

"You're not very modern then."

He laughed. "Nope."

I gulped down my drink. "I suppose you want to hear my confession?"

He laughed again. "Wasn't planning on it."

"You're not trying to convert me?"

He shook his head. "No plans in that direction either."

"You hear Peter's confession."

"That's different: he's taken vows. Look, love isn't a sin—get that idea out of your head."

"I'm not a sinner?"

He shook his head. "The Church got screwed up somewhere at the time of Aquinas."

"St Thomas Aquinas?"

"Yes. A Father of the Church. Well, Augustine was one too. He has a bad press, but he believed erotic love was the way to God, unlike Aquinas, who taught a more sedate route. You've heard of the Greek concept of Agape?"

"I think so—we did it in philosophy."

"That was what St Thomas believed in. It's the love between friends—a more rational love than you and Peter have for each other."

It was anything but rational to be pushing me into bedrooms and bathrooms. "You don't think I'm a sinner then?"

"We're here to love. That's how we find God. But Peter shouldn't be doing this to you."

"It's not that bad."

"Secrecy is always bad."

"Like Blake's poem. *'And his dark secret love / Does thy life destroy.'* "

"Yes, it's destroying you both."

"He expects me to be the strong one. To refuse him. He blames me because I can't."

"He ought to know better. He has no business in a girl's bed-room."

"I'm a Magdalene. The Church sees all women like her. Eve was the original sinner."

"Eve was the mother of the human race."

"What if she had said, 'I don't want this job?' "

"She didn't."

"We'll always be inferior . . ."

"Different, not inferior."

"They downgraded Mary Magdalene, didn't they?"

"What do you mean?"

"She was an apostle—changed into a prostitute."

"I never heard that."

"It boils down to one thing: we'll never be able to stand on the altar as equals."

"There'll be women priests some day. Theologically there's nothing against it. It's just convention."

I stared into my lager. "Yes, but it'll always be God the Father and God the Son. What sex is the Holy Ghost?"

"A spirit is sexually neutral."

"But God is male."

"You're too literal."

"And Mary was a suffering mother. That's the only role for women."

He changed the subject. "If Peter keeps going into your bedroom, he'll have to resign from the order."

I sighed. "He wouldn't like that."

"It'd be a great failure for him."

"You want me to give him up?"

"There's no other solution."

I couldn't pretend that Peter had told me anything about Pat's situation. "Will they ever allow priests to marry?"

He laughed knowingly. "My vocation is for Africa."

"You could bring a wife there."

"I can't leave the priesthood."

"How can you understand life's problems if you're not married?"

He looked sad. "A doctor understands cancer without having experienced it."

We had another drink and sat on in the smoky pub, waiting for

Peter, who never turned up. In the end Pat had to go, because someone was waiting for him.

"I'll see you home."

"I'm OK."

"You're sure?"

"I'm just around the corner."

He gave me his number in case I ever needed help.

Fifteen

MY NEW JOB was checking subscriptions and typing invoices for advertisers. Shane didn't get his commission until they paid up, and antique dealers weren't good at that. They were waiting for people to pay them. I shared an office with Miss Walsh. She must have had a Christian name—everyone does—but I knew her only as Miss Walsh. She was in the telephone book as this, too. Her electric typewriter sounded like a machine-gun, and I sometimes imagined myself ducking a hail of bullets. When she wasn't typing, she was doing her nails, drinking coffee or cleaning the place—she had an obsession with germs.

I tried to chat with her.

"It's a lovely day," I would say.

"I don't need weather bulletins!"

Then she would attack her typewriter, so I gave up.

I had an electric typewriter, too, which I wasn't used to. Unlike Tim's manual, on which I had learnt, this took off any time I touched it, causing hundreds of typing errors. I tried to hide the wasted paper in a basket under my desk, but that was soon full, and the problem was how to hide the evidence of my mistakes from Miss Walsh.

I got the idea of flushing them down the loo. When she wasn't looking, I sneaked the basket into the toilet and pulled the chain on the wadded-up paper. This took a while because the flush didn't work properly. On top of that, there was a nasty damp smell.

When I came out, Miss Walsh was there.

"Are you feeling all right?" she snapped.

I nodded.

"That was a lot of flushing."

I returned to my desk, flustered. She went into the loo after me and sprayed air freshener everywhere, looking daggers at me as she click-clicked back to her desk. I went on typing slowly and carefully, getting through the huge backlog of bills.

At lunchtime Miss Walsh went to the loo again.

"The toilet's blocked," she came out hissing.

I ran in.

There was water all over the floor.

Her eyes widened. "Did you put unsuitable items down?"

I shook my head.

"You're sure?"

"Yes."

Her eyes bored into me. "You know what I'm talking about?"

I knew what she meant, but couldn't say the word. It was too embarrassing, like having to ask the chemist for the discreet package when I was thirteen—it had always seemed to be a male chemist. Then Dunnes Stores liberated Ireland by selling them in supermarkets.

Miss Walsh grabbed the Golden Pages. "We'll have to get a plumber."

"Sorry."

"I'll say you put unsuitable items down."

"Paper," I said.

"Toilet paper?"

I nodded.

"Well . . . it'll be double the cost for an emergency. The editor won't be pleased."

It was a bad start, and things didn't improve.

Despite Amanda, it shocked me when anyone disliked me. I usually related to people and thought myself an agreeable person, but Miss Walsh had a thing about me. Every time I came out of the loo, she ran in and resprayed air freshener. In the end, I was afraid to relieve myself in case she said something nasty—like I had used too much loo paper, or had BO. I should have left after the first day, but didn't, because of the money. I needed the job.

I would have died only for Shane.

One day he was going for lunch, and Miss Walsh was in a worse mood. So I pressed a note into his hand: *"Please don't leave me alone."*

"Take an early lunch," he scribbled back.

"Please!" I mouthed.

But he had to go.

I stayed, fearing another scene, but on that occasion, Miss Walsh was angry with Shane and kept saying that he was "out on the tiles" every night. It was an expression of hers, but particularly upsetting as his wife was expecting a baby. I felt sure it couldn't be true. At lunch hour, I escaped to eat my sandwich in a nearby park.

"I should've warned you," Shane said later over a drink in the pub. "Miss Tight-Twat's jealous of everyone. It's got nuttn' to do with you. We can't keep staff here."

"There've been others before me?"

He nodded. "Needs a good fuckin'."

I was shocked at him saying that, even about Miss Walsh. I had to agree that something was psychologically wrong with her, but was it necessary to be so graphic?

He kept up his habit of bringing in packets of marijuana, wrapped in the same neat way, so I soon refilled the tea tin. Maybe I'd smoke it one day. I still had the rolling tobacco and papers from the last time. Another thing: Shane got extra pay for me. He told the editor I needed travelling expenses, and my wages rose from twenty-five pounds weekly to thirty. Shane was a wheeler-dealer.

So I stayed on at the magazine, trying to ignore Miss Walsh.

At least it stopped me thinking about Peter, although he insisted on ringing me every night. He wouldn't believe me about Miss Walsh and said be nice to her. Nice? My God, he didn't know what a tyrant she was. And he didn't like Shane either. This might have been jealousy, but there was no reason. I did talk about Shane non-stop, but only because he had been to so many places: New York, Mexico City, Barcelona, even Prague.

Shane wanted me to meet his wife, Conchita, who was pushing him to go back to Barcelona because she was worried about the Troubles. Ireland was no country in which to bring up a child. There had been a major train robbery at the end of March, and the IRA was involved. Everyone was nervous of the violence spreading south after the Dublin and Monaghan bombings. I didn't want Shane to leave. I would miss him, and how would I cope with Miss Walsh on my own? Life seemed to be nothing but saying goodbye.

He invited me for dinner at his flat.

The Clontarf bus left from Abbey Street, letting me off outside the old-world, three-storey house at the sea wall. A rash of bells meant that it was divided into about twenty flats and bedsitters. I had brought a bottle of wine—of which I wouldn't partake. I was trying to give up drink. With my mother's drinking record and my Lincoln Inn experience, I concluded that I must have alcoholic genes, so I had made Brigid's mother's famous summer pudding for dessert, leaving out the sherry.

I rang Shane's bell and he came right down the stairs, dressed in paint-splattered denims. His pepper and salt hair was washed and floppy, and through the glass hall door, I saw him ballet-leap down the last few steps.

"Howya, young one?" He hugged me, then took the wine, while I carried the pudding inside. He stood back, looking through me. "Everything hunky-dory?"

I nodded, smiling.

"Yer havin' trouble with yer fella?"

God, did he have second sight or something? The secrecy was killing me.

It was worse now that Brigid had gone and I had no one to confide in. Felicity was too innocent. Besides, it wouldn't be fair to shock a member of the Church of Ireland.

"My flatmate has gone to Kerry," I said.

Shane nodded. "Yer lookin' pale. And yev got thin."

I changed the subject, as he led the way upstairs. "Miss Walsh is getting madder, isn't she?"

"You're a red rag to her."

"Why?"

"Told ya: she needs a man."

Shane went on like this all the time, as if men were all women wanted on earth.

We passed the bathroom on the first landing, which Shane and Conchita shared with other tenants, before coming to their bedsit. It was one large room with a sink and a two-ring cooker in the corner. But it was spotless and painted white, with modern art on the walls. Shane was working on a new canvas—seagulls flocking over a landfill—which I admired.

Conchita had long black hair; her lithe body revealed her bump. She kissed me on both cheeks and pointed to the single bed, covered by a rug, which doubled as a couch. "Sit, Louise."

I wondered how the two of them could sleep in it. As she sat beside me, I asked if I could put my hand on her tummy. It was wonderful to think a child was in there.

"I get kicking this morning," she said in halting English.

I thought something moved. "You want a girl or a boy?"

"Shane wants girl. Me happy with both."

"It's exciting."

"You want children, Louise?"

"Yes, some day."

"You make good mother."

Would I ever be any kind of a mother? Not the way I was going. I was thinking about this as she got some snacks and Shane opened the wine. He drank it, while we had orange juice: Conchita abstained for her pregnancy, and me for safety—which provoked Shane's curiosity.

"You're a puritan, Louise," he said.

Little did he know.

I couldn't explain about my mother or my previous mishaps, so I toasted him with orange juice. Shane told us about his upcoming art exhibition, which was to be held in a Capel Street gallery. The snacks eventually vanished, and since there didn't seem to be any sign of cooking, I wondered if I'd made a mistake about dinner. Maybe they had invited me for an aperitif? It was a continental custom.

Then Conchita asked me to go shopping with her, because she wanted to get things for dinner.

We went to a corner shop. It was in the days before self-service, when shops smelt of bacon and Jacob's biscuits, and assistants in brown coats stood behind a counter. There was a fridge at the front of the shop with frozen food on one side and fresh chickens and meat on the other. Conchita asked for a quarter stone of potatoes, which the assistant went into the back to get. And while he was gone, she picked out a chicken from the fridge and thrust it at me.

"Here!"

"What?"

"Hide it!"

I heard footsteps, so shoved it into my shoulder bag, while Conchita pocketed a pound of butter.

Then the assistant brought out the potatoes in a brown paper bag, and Conchita paid, as if they were the only things needed. I stood with my back to the counter, looking nervously out to the street. Why was Conchita doing this? I had once seen Travellers stealing from a chemist's shop and had said nothing then. I certainly couldn't say anything now. That was the Dublin of the day: everyone was poor, and young people were leaving the country in search of employment. Shane had done the reverse: come back to Erin. But he wasn't properly paid by our "mad bollocks" of an editor. He had to eat; Conchita certainly had to with the baby coming. I swore to myself never to tell Peter what I had done. This would give him something else to tell his friends: he was saving a shoplifter's accomplice.

Sixteen

FELICITY TOLD ME she was getting married and moving home to prepare. It was to be a big wedding in September and I was invited. I would need a new outfit, but I could wear the same dress to Brigid's wedding later in the year.

A flatmate was again a problem. Brigid was right: I could go home to my mother's, but didn't want to. Even then, I knew you couldn't go back in life. In physical terms we can only go forward, like toys with a one-way wind-up key. Even looking back now is suspect, I know, but by writing it all out, I'm trying to understand what happened.

I first met Llewelyn Walker at a gallery opening. She was an American friend of a friend of a friend. Dublin was small in those days, and everyone seemed to know everyone else. There was an actual café called the Grapevine, where I'd heard that Llewelyn now needed a place to live. Although only my age, she was an established painter in Ireland; she did quirky still lifes mainly, some of which had already appeared at art auctions. Her father, a famous New York sculptor, had come to Ireland to work in turf, briquettes with butter and things like that. He exhibited regularly with David Hendriks on the Green and in a famous New York gallery. Now he was breaking up the family home in Howth and returning to the States with a new woman.

Although in awe of Llewelyn, I got the courage to phone and ask if she would share the flat.

To my surprise she made an appointment to view. She was attracted to living in Sandymount because of James Joyce. Stephen D. had walked across the strand to the famous Martello tower in Sandycove. It was in *Ulysses*.

At the arranged hour the bell rang.

I opened the door to a willowy beauty with chestnut hair to her waist. Black-rimmed glasses added an air of severity.

"Am I late?"

"Eh, no."

Although she wore Levis and a boy's hacking jacket, Llewelyn looked right out of *Vogue*. She was strict about the pronunciation of her name too and took an instant dislike to anyone who called her Lou Ellen—Irish people found the Welsh double L difficult—so I was careful.

"This is the sitting room," I said in a businesslike way.

She surveyed the flat in silence.

I walked ahead of her. "It opens to the kitchen."

She stood there, saying nothing.

"A galley kitchen," I said, "with a gas cooker."

Her silence spoke multitudes. Her reaction was so different from Felicity's. Again I saw things through other eyes: the cramped kitchen, the peeling paintwork, the damp bathroom, the rickety, worn-out furniture. The only good thing was the location.

Then she spotted the television set in the corner.

"You watch that?"

My mother had given us the snowy machine with rabbit ears on top. "It only gets RTÉ."

"I can't stand TV."

"I'll move it to my bedroom."

"TV's a waste of time. I'd prefer if you got rid of it."

"OK."

I could bring it to the Simon charity shop or, for the moment, hide it in my room. That way I could look at a programme in bed with the volume low. I liked old cowboys and romantic late night movies. *The Late Late Show* was good on a Saturday night. It was a choice of Gay Byrne or nothing, because Peter was never free, thanks to confessions.

Llewelyn felt the hall walls for damp and said that the place needed painting. "Will the landlady do renovations?"

"I don't know." I was sure she wouldn't.

She made a list in her notebook. "It needs redecorating."

"Miss Pym's never done anything like that."

"It's her job to maintain the place."

"It is?"

"Yes. You pay the rent; she does maintenance. And we'll need new curtains."

True they were at half-mast, but they had come with the place. I doubted we could persuade Miss Pym to change them now. Still, to my equal relief and trepidation, Llewelyn agreed to share, and we arranged that she'd move in the following week, just as her father was departing for the States. In the meantime, I promised to talk to Miss Pym about the redecorating.

Llewelyn came before I had a chance to speak to Miss Pym. I had moved the TV and all my possessions into my room. I suppose it was only fair because I had the biggest one of the three. The rest of the flat was now crammed with Llewelyn's stuff. I had never seen so many things: art materials, wooden sculptures, baskets, all sorts of pens, paintbrushes, paints, paintings, boxes of art books. And stones—she collected stones from a beach in Greystones. There were boxes of them in the hall.

For her first night, I cooked a welcome dinner. Since she was vegetarian, it had to be pasta with a cheese sauce and a salad. Being an American, Llewelyn was up-front about everything. While we were eating, she told me she had just broken up with her boyfriend and asked if I was seeing anyone. It was easier to confide in her than it had been with Felicity. She was more experienced and wouldn't be shocked. So I told her about Peter.

"He's a Bernardite," I explained.

She was puzzled. "What's that?"

"It's a priest."

She looked mildly curious.

"You're not shocked?"

"Why should I be?"

"We're like Héloïse and Abelard."

"The play?"

"No, the actual people." I hesitated. "There's a bit of an impediment."

"He's not good in the sack?"

"No, we can't get married."

She frowned. "Who wants to get married?"

"Well . . ."

"If the sex is good, that's all you need."

Llewelyn was utilitarian and graded men on their performance: good in bed = yes; bad = no.

Seventeen

PETER RESENTED MY new job. I didn't get home till six or seven in the evening now, and he began to hint that I was having some sort of thing with Shane. It was bad enough having one with him. Where would I get the energy? Or the time?

But he didn't believe me.

I tried to understand: he was jealous because I had talked so much about Shane's art and how I admired his dedication. When he had to give up acrobatics, he had tried other things. He wasn't defined by his background or experiences. Life, for Shane, was no brief candle, but a flaming torch. I longed to be like him, to dedicate myself to something. My mother had always wanted me to be a writer, but I knew I couldn't. I didn't have the ideas. But Shane said that I was on the verge of discovering a vocation. I was too interesting to remain a typist. No one had ever said this before. To Nigel I had been an overweight ice cube, and to Peter I was non-reflective and in need of salvation. How he thought he was saving me, I don't know.

One day he turned up at the magazine's office.

I was surprised, but introduced him to Miss Walsh.

"This is Peter. Eh—a friend."

"I won't stay long," he said to her, throwing down his duffle bag and opening his coat. "I was in the neighbourhood and thought I'd drop in to see Louise."

Miss Walsh sniffed and went on typing.

But in a few minutes flat he had thawed her out. The intense blue eyes did their job as he joked about the northside, saying all the best people lived there. She loved it when he started on me, saying that at last I'd found myself a decent job and was getting out of bed in the mornings and working for a living. He implied that I was one of those sixties layabouts. This went down well with Miss Walsh, who thought Dublin 4 types were all unhygienic. It wasn't fair: I had a bath every day.

Miss Walsh made Peter coffee—the better type of Nescafé, kept for herself and the editor, on the rare occasions when he appeared. Shane and I drank the cheap stuff.

I should have said that Peter was a priest from the start, but he wasn't wearing his black clothes that day and could have been any mature student. He had his old sheepskin coat on over a grey, open-neck shirt, grey cords, and the baby blue sweater which Heiner had given him for Christmas. The sweater suited his dark colouring and picked out the blue of his eyes. He had been wearing it when we'd first met.

Miss Walsh wasn't grumpy, for a change, and chatted for a while. Then she went back to her typewriter, which went rat-tat-tat officiously, a hint to get rid of Peter. Any further conversation was impossible. Peter whispered that he had some important news, so I took him into the small damp ante-room, which served as the editor's office.

I whispered, "What is it?"

He grabbed me, laughing. "Just had to see you."

"Is that all?"

"Is that *all,"* he repeated.

"Oh . . . well, come round for dinner tonight."

I planned to get lamb chops on the way home, with maybe some frozen peas and those packet mashed potatoes. No one in the world liked them, except me.

Peter didn't seem satisfied with that. "Is that all you can say?"

"What do you mean?

"Has *it* come?"

"What?"

"Your period?"

He asked this regularly. "No."

He put his head in his hands.

"It's not due yet. Stop obsessing."

"I worry about you. You're sure?"

"I told you. It's every twenty-eight days. It's day twenty since my last."

He started kissing me.

I pulled back.

He touched my breasts.

I mouthed "stop", rolling my eyes towards the main office where the rat-tat-tat was getting angrier. Did Miss Walsh guess what was going on?

Peter wouldn't let me go.

"I had to see you."

That meant he was frustrated.

"I told you," I whispered, "not here. Come round later."

The typing stopped and high-heels click-clicked in our direction. The door was flung open, as Miss Walsh burst in and went straight to the editor's filing cabinet. I jumped back as Peter smiled at her.

She was fussed and red in the face and, although she hadn't

caught us in any compromising position, gave Peter a furtive look. For me, she had the usual face of thunder.

"Sort out these files, Louise!"

"Yes, of course. Peter's just going."

I nodded emphatically at him, swirling my head towards the door, as Miss Walsh fiddled with a stuck drawer, her back to me. She pulled it and the whole thing fell out.

Peter came to the rescue, putting the drawer back. "You need a man around the place."

Miss Walsh softened. "We have one, but he's useless."

That was Shane, who was tramping the streets for ads.

"We have more than a few freeloaders here," she went on.

That was me, who had to have the bathroom checked after use.

Peter made a few more flirtatious jokes, and Miss Walsh went pink with delight. She looked soft and girlish for a change, but after he'd gone, turned her old self on me. "You shouldn't court your boyfriends here."

"He's not a boyfriend."

"What would you call him then?"

"A friend."

"I thought you were going to use the desk."

I ignored this. Again it made me nervous that everyone knew about our affair. We must give off an aura. Otherwise, how could Miss Walsh know? It had been the same with Sandra at the Ecumenical Centre. All that afternoon, Miss Walsh kept up her curious quizzing about Peter. I said he was Canadian, doing a doctorate in Maynooth. It was all true.

"How did you meet him?"

I said it was through a friend, Tim, the editor of *The Trumpet*.

"I'm trying to get into journalism. I write for that paper sometimes."

This impressed her.

She sniffed. "Mammy used to buy it after mass."

"It's a bit old-fashioned."

She didn't agree with this. Everything in the past was better, according to Miss Walsh's view of the universe.

Eighteen

AT EASTER MY mother visited William in London and Llewelyn was away. I spent Good Friday in the flat on my own, finishing the biography of Abelard, borrowed from Canon FitzSimon. There was a canon in Héloïse's story, too: her uncle, Fulbert. In 1115, Abelard took lodgings in his house, and the affair began when he started teaching Héloïse. She was clever and knew several languages in an age when women were uneducated. In his old age, Abelard wrote to a friend:

> *With study as our pretext, we made ourselves wholly free for love, and our lessons provided the furtive privacy love desired; and so, though our books lay open, more words of love prevailed than of instruction, more kisses than precepts. Hands moved more frequently to breasts than to the books. Love turned our gaze more often into each other's eyes than reading kept it on the text. And sometimes, the better to avoid suspicion, I gave her blows, but of love not anger, of affection not wrath, and sweeter they were than any balm. What more can I say? In our passion we omitted none of the steps lovers take, and if there was anything less usual our love might devise, that*

> *too we accomplished. And the less versed we had been in those delights, the more ardently we pursued them, and the less sated we became.*

At least we hadn't been the first: they sounded like us, except for the blows—although I had thrown that shoe at Peter. He had given me books, too, but he acted surprised when I read *The Brothers Karamazov* and the *Confessions of Saint Augustine.* It was a battle to convince him that I had a brain, but I had read nearly all the novels of D. H. Lawrence and Thomas Hardy. I felt a mixture of Lady Chatterley and Tess now. One was sexually liberated, while the other suffered for her sins.

On Easter Saturday, I was invited to midnight mass at the monastery. I wore a hat and was a special guest along with the neighbours and friends of the order. It was a beautiful experience listening to the monks singing, and I prayed for my mother, for the soul of my father, for my brother in London and for peace in Ireland. And us, of course: Peter and me, our non-existent future. But when the priest held up the host, saying "Body of Christ," I thought of Peter's body. I tried to impale him with my stare as he con-celebrated, looking all holy in a white surplice. Afterwards there was a gathering with tea and sandwiches. I chatted to Heiner, Johanna and a couple of their daughters, until Peter joined us dressed in his medieval black and white habit. I had never seen it before, and he reminded me of a figure from a holy picture. Heiner probably thought I was being saved again, but I didn't care. I felt dipped in grace or something. It was the same feeling as after my father's death when I knew his spirit was watching over me.

Easter didn't do anything to reform Peter. The ceremony hadn't affected him in the way it had me. He started obsessing about my period again.

He phoned daily, always first thing in the morning. "Well, has it come?"

"What?" I was never properly awake.

"It's flowing strongly?"

"No . . . it hasn't come yet."

"Oh, my God. You're sure?"

"Yes!"

"Don't shout. Someone might hear."

"I'm not shouting, and there's no one here."

"Isn't the landlady upstairs?"

"She's gone to work."

He was paranoid about people knowing. A pregnancy would surely make them ask questions. Yet nothing would persuade him to use a condom or let me use the spermicidal jelly I had bought. He still insisted on *coitus interruptus.* He didn't care about the law of the land. No, contraception was against the teaching of the Holy Roman Catholic Church. It allowed the "safe period" only, where you took your temperature. I could never manage that, because I didn't have the proper thermometer. It was too expensive. Instead, Peter kept on with his method.

He said it was safe and not to worry.

"Was that good?" he'd ask. "Was it good for you?"

I always said yes, because it was.

After Easter my period *was* late. I wasn't too worried, since it had happened before. Once when I was teaching in the tech, I had missed for six months. I knew I wasn't pregnant then—you can't drown if there's no water. When I mentioned it to the head of the English department, who had befriended me, she had stopped talking and stared. "It's eh—just stress," I stammered, realising what she must have thought. This brought more funny looks. But pregnancy had never occurred to me then, and it didn't now.

But Peter became frantic because I was late.

"Any sign of it?" he asked.

"Nothing. Sorry."

A heavy silence. Then, "Oh, my God."

"Listen, it's only two weeks late."

"You've never missed before."

"I have. Often." I told him about the teaching episode.

"You weren't pregnant?"

"No! Do you think I have secret children?"

"There's no need to shout," Peter hissed into the receiver.

"I'm not shouting!" Then I calmed myself. "It'll come next month. So stop worrying."

"I always worry about you, Louise."

I hung up and went back to bed.

By the time I knew, I was two months gone. I figured I had got pregnant at the time of our tryst in the Irish School of Ecumenics. Although Peter still claimed I wasn't a real Christian, we had certainly unified on that occasion.

Our family doctor looked at me over his glasses. "I'm afraid the test was positive."

I was stunned.

"I'm pregnant?"

He nodded. "Very."

"You're sure?"

"There's no doubt."

He gave me the address of an adoption agency and asked if my mother knew. I had known the doctor all my life and asked him not to tell her. My mother wasn't the narrow-minded type, and I knew she wouldn't buy me a suitcase and a ticket to England. I just wanted to break it to her myself.

I rang Peter with the news. The telephone was easier.

"Oh, my God," he groaned.

I pictured the despair on his face.

"You're sure?"

"I am."

"We'll talk this evening," he said, hanging up.

When Héloïse got pregnant, Abelard married her secretly, but they ended up apart because of her family's act of revenge. Their child, Astralabe, was brought up by others in a monastery. I would bring up my own child, although being an unmarried mother would be difficult. I didn't expect any help from Peter because of his vow of poverty.

He came to the flat after dinner, with two bottles of wine from the monastery cellar. Pouring us a glass each, he shook his head without speaking, as if someone were dead or he'd heard the worst news of his life.

I didn't feel like drinking or talking.

He sipped his wine, eventually breaking the silence. "I've thought about this. I know you want an abortion."

I was too shocked to say anything.

"It's wrong, but I can't stop you."

I didn't answer.

"You're young. You won't want to tie yourself down."

I was staring into my glass.

"I suppose you'll go to London?" he went on.

What was he saying? "Eh—no."

He gulped his wine, alarm in his voice. "What?"

"I'm not going anywhere."

"You're not?"

The thought had never occurred to me. I wasn't against abortion for others. I believed in choice, but I couldn't do it myself. My mother would help me to look after the baby. After all, she had always wanted to be a grandmother. Having deprived her of my white wedding, I couldn't deprive her of a grandchild.

Peter was calm. "You'll have the baby adopted then?"

I shook my head. "I'm keeping it."

He swallowed. "Adoption might be a better solution."

"I don't think so."

"It would be taken care of."

"That'd be like Astralabe."

"Astralabe?"

"Héloïse's baby."

"Oh . . . Ast*ro*labe."

"It's Ast*ra*labe in the book I read. He was sent away to a monastery."

"I can't bring up a child. I have a contemplative vocation."

I had heard nothing else *in saecula saeculorum.*

He raked back his hair. "It'll ruin me if the truth gets out."

That got to me. "Don't be such a wanker!"

He paled. "That's bad language, Louise."

"It's the vernacular."

"Show some respect."

"You show some respect! For me. Stop thinking of yourself."

He looked about to explode. "You shouldn't call a priest a wanker."

"A wanker is an agent noun."

"A what?"

"A noun denoting the doer of an action—as in builder, plumber, gardener."

He raked his hair again. "Even if I did marry you, there'd be a fortune to repay the order."

"They've lent you money?"

"They've paid my fees, my degree."

Then he dug into his pocket, took out a twenty pound note and handed it to me.

"What's that for?"

"You'll need money."

I threw it at him.

"Look, calm down."

"You *are* a wanker!"

He put his hands to his ears. "*Please,* Louise."

I was incensed. "I have a job, and I earn money from journalism." An overstatement, but I was determined to keep trying.

"You won't be able to work if you're having a baby."

"It's not a disease."

Peter took out his pipe and started filling it.

"Everyone has to be born. The world doesn't stop," I said.

In the end I cooked my usual meal of steak, mash and frozen peas because Peter said he was hungry and something to eat would make us feel better. But he didn't have much of an appetite, and neither did I.

Then the morning sickness started: it was relentless but a connection to the life within me, making itself felt. A baby was something tangible, something Peter couldn't take away from me. I would have a piece of him at least. I didn't tell my mother, fearful of the consequences of upsetting her. I was afraid to confide in Llewelyn and missed Brigid more and more.

Despite being lonely and worried about the future, I kept going to work as usual. I knew something was wrong when Miss Walsh gave me her mad little smile.

"You're a dark horse."

"What do you mean?"

"Is *Father* Fanning planning to leave his order for you?"

I looked at her, stunned.

"Your friend's a priest!"

As bad luck would have it, Miss Walsh had gone on a day retreat which Peter had conducted. He facilitated women's groups, and this was to a Child of Mary sodality in a northside church.

She feigned sympathy. "Why didn't you tell me he was a priest?"

"Did I have to?"

"You could have said something."

"You don't go round saying you're an office manager."

"A priest is different."

"Why?"

"Once a priest, always a priest." She attacked her typewriter, making the usual machine-gun noise. Then stopped. "My faith means a lot to me. I wouldn't have thought you'd be interested in religion."

"Father Fanning's saving me."

"Saving you?"

"From eternal regret."

"What's that?"

"Not seeing the face of God."

It was true in a way, but she rat-tatted angrily on, unconvinced.

I didn't see Peter for a week, and when he came to the flat next, he was still upset.

He put his head in his hands. "You're trying to force my hand."

I kept cool. "I'm not forcing anything."

"It's no fun bringing up a child on your own."

"I'll have my mother."

He was shocked. "You've told her?"

I shook my head. "Not yet."

I couldn't explain that she wasn't stable and that the news might push her back to alcoholism. I had to pick my moment to tell her.

He scanned my figure. "You won't be able to hide it soon. What about your flatmate? Does Llewelyn know?"

"I've told no one."

Again I tried to explain that I couldn't do what everyone else wanted. For once, I was doing what *I* wanted. He could take it or leave it. So he grabbed his duffle bag and left.

Then I began to lose confidence and fear set in. Why hadn't I met a man who would stand by me? It had been so different for Brigid and Felicity, who had caring boyfriends. Why didn't Peter include me in his future? I had been a fool to love him, but I couldn't help it.

Llewelyn found me sitting in the dark one evening.

"What's up?" she asked, putting on the kettle.

"Nothing."

"You look tragic."

I decided to tell her. "It's an Irish situation."

"Oh?"

She'd have to know when the baby started showing. "I'm pregnant."

She wrinkled her nose in horror. "What!"

I nodded. "I'm afraid so."

"Peter?"

I nodded again.

"He can't marry me."

"You don't have to *marry.*" She hesitated. "Didn't you take precautions?"

I shook my head. "He wouldn't hear of it."

"You Irish are all the same. What's so terrible about contraception?"

"He's a priest, Llewelyn."

"I don't care what he is! He shouldn't have knocked you up. Now you'll have to go to London. Who's going with you?"

I said nothing.

She opened her diary and began checking dates. "I have an exhibition coming up, but I can take a weekend off. I'll see about booking a flight for Saturday. Can you get off work?"

I had only once flown to London. The whole country was kept in a state of siege by Aer Lingus. "No."

"You'll have to ring in sick."

Again I said no.

"I'll ring in for you."

"No!"

"You'll have to tell them if you're in London."

"I don't want an abortion."

"What?" She was horrified. "You're not considering *having* it?"

"I know it's not very modern."

"What does your family say?"

"I haven't told them yet. My brother's working in London. I know my mother won't mind. She's always talking about being a granny. She'll be glad to help me."

"She wants to be a grandmother?" Llewelyn paused. "Look, the question is: do you want to be a mother?"

"I think so."

She flicked back her beautiful hair, contemplating this. "I suppose it's selfish of me, but I'm not having any children."

"It's not selfish."

"I'm an artist. I don't want to waste any time."

"You've got as much time as anyone else."

"Every life is too short."

Llewelyn kept saying that Peter should face up to his responsibilities. She wanted to punch him for being a prick. And, although she would stand by me, she wanted to hit me on the side of the head for not using a contraceptive. I had to wake up and realise what I was doing to myself by having the baby or having anything more to do with Peter. I agreed, but the horse had bolted now. Peter had been irresponsible, but what could he do? He believed in the Catholic Church's teaching and bishops dressing up like the Ku Klux Klan. He didn't want to leave the order, and I assumed he would have to if news of the baby got out. That's why he was so against my keeping it. But it wasn't right to say that he didn't care about me. He was just naturally upset at the idea of being a father.

All this time Llewelyn was arguing with Miss Pym about the redecoration of the flat. She wanted the whole place repainted and the damp problem fixed. Miss Pym wouldn't budge: she kept insisting that the responsibility for the interior was *ours,* and the exterior *hers.* It was in our contract, and she could get ten people in the morning to replace us.

So Llewelyn said we'd do the decoration ourselves. The paint was peeling, so we scraped it off, then bought new tins in Sandymount Green and set to work, not stopping until the living room was a pristine white.

After we had finished, I climbed the ladder to get a patch we had missed on the ceiling.

"Be careful on that ladder," Llewelyn said.

"Don't worry." But in reaching upward, I got a sudden dizzy spell and fell.

There was a terrible crash, and for a minute I saw stars.

"Are you OK?" Llewelyn was standing over me.

"I'm fine," I laughed, looking at the paint everywhere, "but the carpet's ruined."

"That carpet's had it anyway. I'm worried about you."

I was unhurt, except for my arm, which would come out in a purple bruise. I had always bruised easily, but it would mend.

In the middle of that night I got bad pains in my lower stomach. I had had my appendix out—what on earth could this be? It never occurred to me what was happening. When I went to the toilet, it was full of blood. Although pregnant, I had got my period. How was that?

Llewelyn heard me moaning and got up.

"A miscarriage," she announced, looking into the bowl.

I stared at the blood. "You're sure?"

"I'm sure." She flushed the chain.

"Don't!"

But it was too late.

Llewelyn stood there awkwardly. "I'm sorry. It was a reflex action."

"It's OK," I said, swallowing hard.

"Listen, it might be for the best."

I didn't answer.

"I'll call an ambulance."

One came and took me to hospital. All the way, I felt guilty for climbing the ladder and falling. Why had I done it? Why had Llewelyn insisted on painting? But I couldn't blame her. The baby was gone, and it had been my own stupid fault.

Nineteen

THEY WERE SYMPATHETIC at the hospital, saying it often happened with a first pregnancy. A miscarriage was part of the natural process of weeding out unhealthy embryos. There was no way of preventing it, once it had started. In more than 60 per cent of cases, there was a problem with the way genetic material from the egg and the sperm combined, and there was no reason for this, other than bad luck. It had not been caused by stress or lack of rest, and had been probably nothing to do with falling off the ladder. Was that true or were they trying to make me feel better?

I rang Peter and told him.

"It's God's will," he said.

He sounded so matter-of-fact, it made me feel worse, and I wept into the receiver.

"What is it, love?"

It was the second time he had called me that. "You're glad, aren't you?"

"No . . . I'm sorry, love."

I choked back tears.

"Are you still there, Louise?"

"You call yourself *Father.*"

He said nothing.

"But you don't know the meaning of the word."

"You need to rest, Louise."

After we hung up, I wept again for our child and all the children we might have had. Another patient consoled me that it would be different next time, but I didn't want a next time. Ever. I was discharged after a D&C. They said I'd be sore for a while, and I was, but it was nothing to the pain inside me.

I didn't want sex again either.

For the moment that was OK, because they said not to do it for a month. But the pregnancy had been a definite turn-off, so we just watched TV when Peter came round. We saw one film with Henry Fonda about an American who robbed stores to support his family. "The poor bastard," Peter muttered, and I knew he didn't want any responsibilities. Least of all me and a baby.

Yet I kept on loving him.

Was I under a spell?

Peter tried to give me up again, but we soon reverted to our old ways. So I made an appointment to get the pill at the Family Planning Clinic. Meantime, I wasn't taking any more chances, so I found the condoms in a drawer. But Peter still refused to use them, insisting that his method worked. He had the power to pull back at the vital moment. And condoms were unmanly, besides being against his religion.

When I argued, he announced that he had never got anyone pregnant before. Withdrawal had always worked in the past, with Stella and everyone else. I knew all about her from Peter. How she had pined for him after he had gone to the monastery, and how she couldn't accept his vocation. Who would he tell about me?

Then it dawned on me what he was saying.

"You think I got pregnant by someone else?"

"I never said that."

I was furious. "You did!"

"Louise, please! You're putting words into my mouth. I said it had always worked before. I slipped up this time, that's all."

My anger brought tears.

He held me in his arms. "Now stop this."

"I can't."

"What is it?"

"I lost our baby."

He frowned. "I know. I know . . . but . . . maybe it was for the best."

How could anyone be so cold?

"A baby was flushed down the loo." I caught my breath. "The *loo!* You're an absolute bastard."

This time he didn't say anything about the bad language, but lit his pipe worriedly, going through the usual ritual of packing it and letting out mushrooms of aromatic smoke. "It was a miscarriage."

"The Catholic Church says it was a human being."

"Look, *I'm* the theologian. Leave the Catholic Church to me!"

"Why didn't they give me the rest of it?"

He blew out more smoke. "The rest of it?"

"The body."

"You had a miscarriage. There was nothing else."

"I could have buried it properly. I'd have had somewhere to mourn."

"It was human tissue, Louise. The Church's teaching might well change with regard to embryos. Saint Thomas thought ensoulment didn't take place until a few weeks after conception."

"That was in ancient times."

"He's still a Father of the Church."

I thought about this. "I don't know if it was a boy or a girl."

"It wasn't either."

His matter-of-factness was upsetting.

"It would have had to be buried *outside* the church grounds," I said.

"What?"

"If it had died before being baptised. The Catholic Church always did that to unbaptised babies. They were rejected in life and death."

"Louise, calm down. It wasn't a baby!"

"It's a shitty Church." The thought of all those little ones choked me up. "Why are there no requiems for babies?"

"You're overreacting."

"*I'm* overreacting? That's a good one!"

He put his arms around me. "I'm sorry. You're right. I haven't considered your feelings."

I was crying.

"Forgive me, Louise?"

I said nothing.

"Please, love."

I stopped crying. "What's limbo like?"

He sighed. "Peter Abelard thought up that. Thanks to him, the Vatican decreed that unbaptised babies didn't go to hell, but to limbo. It was believed they would feel no pain there, but no happiness either—because they wouldn't be able to see God."

"That was big of them!"

"The doctrine isn't taught now."

"But it's in the catechism."

"It's dated." Peter went on trying to console me. "Listen, miscarriages happen every day."

"Couldn't you bless the toilet?"

He looked alarmed. "The toilet?"

"That's where it went. You can do a baptism. A small ceremony."

He was firm. "Louise, you're having some sort of breakdown. There was no baby."

"There you go again. It *was* a baby. A potential baby."

He held up his hands. "OK, OK."

"It can be a baptism of desire or something. I remember that from catechism class."

The room had filled with smoke. "Well, theologically . . . I suppose, there's no reason I can't do something."

I wiped my eyes.

"You'll do it?"

He pocketed his pipe, sighing. "Have you decided on a name?"

"Astralabe, after Héloïse's baby."

"An astrolabe was a medieval instrument to show the positions of the sun and the stars. It was used to guide mariners."

"That's lovely. We need guidance too."

"It'd be like calling a baby Typewriter."

"I want it."

"What about Jean—that's for a boy or a girl."

Astralabe was some connection with those two lovers nearly nine hundred years ago. We argued for a bit, but Peter agreed in the end, so we had a small ceremony that evening. I put candles in the bathroom, and he got his gear from the monastery, a sort of neck stole and a missal. He prayed over the toilet. "I bless you, Astralabe, in the name of the Father and the Son and the Holy Ghost."

I was happy.

"Now, how's that?"

I was too emotional to answer.

He closed his missal, took off the stole and kissed my cheek. "I couldn't love you if you weren't so bloody daft."

My child was a spirit, journeying through the underworld of the Dublin sewers, out to the freedom of the Irish Sea, then the wide salty oceans. Maybe it would find a friendlier world than this one. Maybe it would guide my spirit too. I hoped we would meet in another life. If the Catholic Church was right, we would. According to them, a life was a life from conception. That was some consolation. Afterwards Peter and I ended up in bed together, but I was too upset for anything, so we fell asleep.

Then I discovered my mother drinking. It was another Sunday lunchtime. I had been afraid to tell her about my pregnancy and miscarriage, in case she told the Canon or everyone in Dublin, but I didn't think it necessary to keep Shane's marijuana a secret: especially the detail that he grew it in his hot press. My mother knew I didn't even smoke cigarettes, so she would surely think it funny that he supplied me. After all, she was a reformed drinker, and alcohol was far worse than harmless grass, which was good for you, according to the thinking of the day.

To my amazement, she threatened to ring the guards.

"I'll have him deported."

"You can't. He's Irish."

"So what?"

She stormed upstairs and came down a while later with a letter she had written, reporting Shane for growing illegal substances.

I grabbed it. "You're not posting that."

"Give it back, Louise."

"He can't be deported from his own country."

"What about his wife then?" my mother fumed.

"What about her?"

"She's Spanish."

I said they were legally married.

Then I knew the truth. It was the sort of crazy thing she did when she had a break. "You've been drinking again."

This enraged her. "How dare you!"

"You have."

"I have not!"

We went back and forth, as always: *You have! I haven't! How dare you accuse me?*

But irrational anger at my friends was a typical symptom, and in the end she admitted the truth, giving me the empty naggin bottle from the bin. I stayed overnight, sleeping in my old bedroom to prevent her from topping up. All night she ranted, threatening to report Shane for the "corruption" of her daughter. It was wearing me out.

Next morning she was penitent.

I brought her a cup of tea before leaving for work.

"My God, I feel like death," she moaned from her bed.

I said nothing.

"I'm sorry, Louise."

I held in my anger.

"I don't deserve a daughter like you."

I remembered my hangover after meeting Peter. I wasn't any saint either. "Drink your tea. It'll make you feel better."

"Why will I never learn?"

"Promise to go to Alcoholics Anonymous?"

She nodded. "There's a meeting tonight in Ranelagh."

"Why did you break?"

"I'm sorry, darling."

"But why?"

"I was worried about you."

"What're you worried about?"

"That creepy priest. He was oily."

"It's all over with him," I lied.

"Is it?"

I nodded.

She looked disappointed. "I don't have to worry about him?"

"No, I took your advice. I told him he'd have to go on a retreat, so he broke it off."

She looked unconvinced. "Just like that."

I nodded. "Yes."

"You're telling me the truth?"

"Mum, take care of yourself. Stop worrying about me."

Looking hurt, she sipped her tea.

Why had I told her about Peter? Thank God, I hadn't made the mistake of mentioning my pregnancy and miscarriage.

Twenty

MISS WALSH HATED me more and more.

Although she hadn't guessed why I was off work after the miscarriage, she'd been suspicious when I had had to spend more time than ever in the loo, with morning sickness. The usual spraying ceremony had always taken place afterwards, and she was still doing it, although I was back to normal now. I felt like one of those prisoners, deloused in concentration camps. I still had a bath every morning and was always careful about hygiene. Why was she behaving like this? It might be jealousy about Peter, but she had disliked me long before finding out about him.

I hadn't been the only one to fall for Peter's looks and wouldn't be the last. Miss Walsh was obviously smitten. She kept quizzing me. Where was he stationed? And why had he come to Ireland? And who was he doing a dissertation on? I explained it was a Dutch theologian who was into ecumenism, but she hadn't heard of him.

Then Peter appeared at my flat one night, ashen-faced.

"Well, the shit's hit the fan."

I'd never seen him like this, not even when I was pregnant.

"What is it?"

"I've been called for an interview with the master of studies."

"He knows about me?"

Peter nodded. "Someone has written an anonymous letter."

"God!"

"I'll be sent away. It's my own fault."

For once he wasn't blaming me: that was a change.

But he turned on me. "Who've you told?"

Neither my mother nor the Canon knew Peter's full name. "Eh, no one."

"Someone else knows."

"Miss Walsh?" I suggested.

"You told her?"

"No, but she knows you're a priest."

He put his head in his hands. "She's the type to write a poison-pen letter."

I agreed. Miss Walsh was full of poison.

"She told me she attended a retreat you gave."

"A day retreat? At Raheny?"

"Didn't you notice her?"

"No . . . there were a lot of women. I need your support, Louise."

"Of course."

"Otherwise, I'll be chucked out of the order. Laicised. I won't be able to finish my doctorate."

Nervously I made coffee. Miss Walsh hadn't guessed about my pregnancy, I was sure. She had told on us because she was jealous of our love, although since the miscarriage, we were again trying to give each other up. It was the story of our life: on, off, on, off.

He sat down and lit up. "He'll throw canon law at me."

"There's a law about us?"

"The Church has a legal system. I'll have to see my confessor, then shun you."

I coughed as the room filled with smoke. "Shun me?"

He blew out more. "I'm afraid so."

"You mean walk past me in the street?"

He nodded. "Something like that."

"Could we meet secretly?"

"Sorry, love. You have to understand the reality of the situation."

"I told you: it's a cliché."

He puffed irritably. "OK, OK."

"Will you shun me for ever?"

"I could never shun you."

"You'll only pretend?"

"Yes." He said nothing for a moment. Then, "Thank God, there's no child."

"Stop saying that!"

"Louise, calm down. A child would have messed things up with the order."

Peter's worry about the order got to me. But he was so upset, I didn't say anything more. That night he left early, as usual, so I fell asleep on my own. I had lost the baby, and if Peter were sent away I'd lose him too. I still couldn't face life without him.

The next day I confronted Miss Walsh. She was doing her nails at her desk as I came in. The red varnish mingled with remover took my breath away.

Miraculously I had lost all fear. "I know what you've done."

She smiled madly, screwing the top back on the varnish.

I hated her.

"OK, so you found out Peter is a priest," I continued, "but you could be wrong about an affair."

She still didn't answer.

"It wasn't a Christian thing to do."

This brought a cool response. "I don't know what you're talking about."

"Yes, you do! You wrote a letter to his superior about Father Fanning and me."

She looked outraged.

"How dare you say that!"

"How dare *you!*"

She put her nail stuff in a drawer and banged it shut. "You shouldn't be carrying on with him anyway."

"And you should mind your own business. You're not Christian."

This incensed her and she started shouting, "You're a whore! Out on the tiles every night!"

"What tiles?"

"I can smell it off you!"

"What?"

"Sex!"

"You're mad. You've smells on the brain."

She put paper into her typewriter, jamming it. She was shaking with anger, so I said nothing more.

After a bit, I broke the silence. "You need psychiatric treatment, you know."

Her eyes bulged. "How *dare* you!"

"I'm telling you for your own good."

She looked about to cry. "Why do you say that?"

"It isn't healthy to be always smelling things."

"I've had a difficult life since Mammy died."

"When was that?"

"Ten years ago. She died in her sleep. I found her. My sister went to Australia years ago. She's never come back."

I didn't blame the sister.

She started crying. "I'm all alone in the world."

I'd have gone, too, as far away as possible. I watched her crying, saying at last, "Look, I'm sorry about your mother."

"I miss Mammy so much."

She was howling again.

"Your sister will come home, if you ask her."

This softened her. She dabbed her eyes with a hanky. "I didn't tell on Father Fanning; although, mind you, I suspected the worst."

I wasn't letting her away with it. "You did!"

She shook her head.

"You wrote a letter."

She kept denying it, but I didn't believe her. She was trying to ruin Peter, and I told her so to her face. She cried again, but I didn't care: it was an act to make me feel bad. We started shouting at each other and kept it up until Shane came in and calmed us down. He took me for a drink after work.

"Ye hafta ignore her, Louise," he said.

I nodded, then asked him to tell me the truth about something.

He was curious. "What?"

"You'll be honest?"

He nodded.

"Do I smell?"

He laughed aloud.

"Of course not! Where'd you get that idea?"

"Miss Walsh is always spraying the loo with air freshener."

"She's a bitch!"

I couldn't argue with that.

"If I wasn't married to Conchita, you'd be top of my list, Louise. Deffo."

I didn't know what to say.

"You're always nicely turned out. I noticed it the first day. I said to meself, "That's a smart young one. Don't mind that bloody witch!"

I promised to try and ignore her. Then in the intimacy of the pub and under the spell of a pint, I told Shane about Peter. How I was in love and it was so painful because he was a priest. I didn't dare mention the miscarriage.

He got me another drink. "Ah, sure, they're all shysters in the Catholic Church. You know why they have celibacy?"

"It's in the Gospel, I suppose."

"It isn't. Saint Peter was married. A few of the other apostles were. Priests were allowed to marry in the Middle Ages. It's a man-made rule to protect the Church's property."

I frowned. Peter didn't own anything. "Property?"

"Sure, marriage is a contract for the transfer of property. A married clergy would fuck that up. The priest's house would have to go to the wife."

I'd never heard of this reason for celibacy.

He looked at me kindly. "Louise, you're like a character in a novel."

"What do you mean?"

"Other people don't love like that."

"Like what?"

"So purely."

"You love Conchita."

He hesitated. "I do, but . . ."

I was shocked by his hesitation. "You're not faithful?"

Then he told me he hadn't always been, but that they had worked things out when she became pregnant. Now things were great between them. That was a relief. I envied their ordinary life. That was all I wanted: to share my life with someone ordinary. Someone who came home to dinner every evening, who would read the paper and take me to the pub now and again. A man like my father.

Peter asked me to see his master of studies. I said I would, but what was I to say? He said that was up to me, but to remember he could be laicised because of Miss Walsh's treachery. I still daydreamed that we'd marry and go somewhere on the missions. A foreign place, far from Holy Catholic Ireland. Meanwhile, I couldn't go on working with a mad woman who might murder me, so I quit my job at the magazine and waited in some trepidation for my interview with Peter's superior.

Twenty-one

THE HOUSE OF Studies was a cold granite institution, flanked by newly budding trees. Spring was in the air, and a chilly wind blew my hair about as I walked up the avenue. On one side young men were playing football in a field. They did not shout to each other, or whistle and catcall me. Instead they kicked the ball, ignoring me. It was so different from my experiences of visiting my brother's school or walking past men on building sites or roadworks. I assumed these were baby priests, and women were a temptation. We were the fallen sex, the children of Eve who had been responsible for Adam's sin.

I was nervous, but determined to save Peter. I remembered what his friend Pat had said about the need to say mass. It would never work out between us. Despite studying Hans Küng, Peter believed in all that dogma—papal infallibility and an unmarried clergy—although you would never think it by his behaviour. The Catholic Church was unforgiving of any dissent. We were asked to believe impossible things: the pope was infallible, Mary had been born immaculate, then assumed into heaven without the inconvenience of death. Jesus gave us his body and blood in the form of bread and wine, before rising from the dead.

Abelard had been castrated by Héloïse's family for the crime of love. Thousands had been burnt alive during the Inquisition for questioning the faith. And Galileo had been forced to recant his discovery that the earth went around the sun, and not vice versa. All his books had been burnt, and he had been placed under house arrest. It had taken 350 years for the Vatican to apologise. Things hadn't changed much. What would they do to Peter for loving me? As well as a vow of chastity, he had taken one of obedience. He had renounced his own will and promised to obey his superior, whose authority came directly from God.

I knew he wouldn't be burnt at a stake, or cast down to hell for ever. After all, it was the twentieth century. But he wouldn't be allowed to say mass; he wouldn't be a special representative of Jesus, whose yoke was sweet and burden light; he couldn't save souls or forgive sins; he wouldn't have anointed hands and would have to renounce his vocation and get a job like everyone else. They could never stop him being a Catholic, but it would kill him to be silenced and defrocked.

What would the master of studies say? Would he blame me for everything? But who had betrayed us? No matter how she denied it, it had to be Miss Walsh. She was the only person I knew with a vindictive nature. Couldn't she have minded her own business for once? The world was full of busybodies, people deprived of love by a cold-hearted religion. It had made them nasty and, in her case, mentally ill. Her obsessions couldn't be healthy. I wasn't sorry about telling her to get help.

Stone steps led to an institutional hall door. One, two, three, four, five, six, seven, all good children go to heaven, I counted, going up. One of my mother's infatuations had been the priest headmaster of my brother's school. It was crazy to remember that now. She had been madly in love with him, but when my brother left for the senior school, the priest had met her for the pictures, telling her it had to end. She had asked me to write and say not to be so mean. I did, so he had written back, explaining that nothing improper had happened between them. I always remember he had signed it *"With renewed good wishes"*. It had seemed so sophisticated that for years I had signed letters like that. It showed what an idiot I had been. But my mother had been crazy, asking a child to write such a letter. I was only eleven and didn't understand.

The hall door was forbidding.

I rang a bell.

A granite saint frowned down from the overhead niche. He was like some stone bishop, wagging a frozen finger with one hand and holding a staff in the other. Was it Saint Patrick casting the snakes out of Ireland? There was a crucifix on the roof and a chapel with a stained-glass window at one end. I imagined endless rows of chanting black-robed priests inside. I had seen them at Easter. How did they live without sexual love? Had they entered out of school like the boys playing football? Had they been indentured by their families to get an education? Maybe it was easy to renounce love at that age, but could they promise to remain celibate all their lives? Did they know what they were renouncing? How did they know that they wouldn't one day meet a woman in need of a taxi?

But it was dawning on me: priests *didn't* manage without love. How could they? How could any human being unless they were desiccated old men? What was it all for? Hadn't Peter confessed to Pat, only to be asked for forgiveness in return? Wasn't the celibacy of the Church a vast hypocrisy, one priest forgiving the next for the crime of love? Like a game of tip and tig?

An old brother in a stained habit opened the door, out of breath.

"I'm Louise O'Neill," I said. "I've an appointment with Father Power."

He expected me. "Yes, my dear. Come this way."

He heaved the door shut, and I followed him into the brown, square hall, smelling of beeswax polish, then down a darker corridor to an uncomfortable reception room. Peter called this house his home, but there was nothing homely about it. A glass bookcase took up one wall, and in the middle was a round conference table with hard, straight-backed chairs.

"Take a seat. I'll ring Father Power's bell."

After he left, it clanged three times, then once. The system of communication reminded me of smoke signals in cowboy movies.

There was a crucifix on one wall.

Thou hast conquered, O pale Galilean; the world has grown grey from thy breath.

On the other wall, there was a picture of Jesus pointing to His bloodstained heart. The eyes followed me around the room, silently accusing. A voice came into my head: "You've pierced my Sacred Heart, Louise." I stared back: my heart was broken, too. I put on lipstick and tidied my hair, checking my reflection in the glass bookcase. My hair was wild after being washed, and I combed out the tangles as I read the book titles. They were mainly ancient hardbacks: the lives of saints. It didn't look as if anyone ever disturbed them. At school retreats, a nun had read books like that aloud. All my memories of religion were cold and unfriendly. As I sat nervously at the table, I remembered being counselled by a priest after leaving school. I was sent by a nun because I said I never wanted to get married and never wanted a boyfriend. That time I also sat at a table and looked down to see that the priest had exposed himself. It had put me off sex even more, but, although young, I knew that the man was lonely. It was a thing young girls had to put up with. I just pretended it wasn't happening and had never told anyone, not even my mother and, least of all, the nun who had sent me. She wouldn't have believed me anyway.

Now I was again to be alone with a stranger.

I wanted to go to the loo.

After a while, a small, bespectacled, white-haired man in a habit opened the door. I stood up and we shook hands. He pulled a chair out and sat opposite to me.

"Thank you for coming, Louise."

"It's OK," I said.

He came straight to the point.

"I received this letter, saying you and Father Peter are in a relationship. Is it true?" He cocked his head, waiting for an answer.

I felt weak. The letter was written on lilac notepaper. "No, Father."

He peered at me, surprised. "But he's a regular visitor to your flat?"

"He has come, eh, once or twice."

"He's been seen sitting outside, waiting for you to return."

I tried to see the letter, but couldn't. The notepaper suggested that it was from a woman: a man would never use that colour. But Miss Walsh didn't know about Peter sitting on the windowsill. Could it have been Miss Pym? Had she seen him? Would she even care? Love wasn't a sin for a Protestant. Catholics alone were famous for sins of the flesh. I had never heard Nigel mention such things, and besides Felicity, he was the only other Protestant I knew. I didn't know what religion Llewelyn was. Probably none.

"Before I take any action against Father Fanning, I wanted to hear your side of the story." His eyes bored into me.

The word "action" alarmed me. "Peter, eh—Father Peter—was advising me, Father."

"Advising you?"

"Yes, helping me."

He held up the letter. "It couldn't help you, if there's any truth in this."

"It—eh . . ." Then the solution just came to me. "I have a drink problem, Father."

Peter had told people that. And, thanks to my mother, I knew all about alcoholism. How it necessitated going to AA and following the Twelve Steps.

Father Power looked relieved. "My poor child."

"When we met, I was drunk."

"You were? Well, I must say, that puts a different slant on things." He tucked his hands in his habit.

"I was upset because I'd lost my job. Father Peter brought me home. He's been advising me ever since."

"Advising you?"

I nodded. "Helping me give up drink."

"Well, in that case. . . . You're unhappy, my child?"

I nodded. "I am."

"And have you joined Alcoholics Anonymous?"

"I have," I lied.

"You go to meetings regularly?"

"I do. I'm trying to go every day. It's a bit hard with my job, but I follow the Twelve Steps."

He nodded. "Have you thought of joining the Pioneers?"

"I took the pledge for my confirmation."

"Good child."

"Unfortunately, it didn't work."

He shook his head. "You could rejoin. Are you saying your prayers?"

I nodded. "Sometimes, eh . . . not enough."

"God will help us if we ask Him. If you ask your Father for bread, will He give you a stone?"

I had a flat full of Llewelyn's stones.

"I've asked Father Peter not to see you again."

My heart jumped. "Oh . . ."

"Your flat is a temptation for him. It might be an occasion of sin."

"I know."

His eyes narrowed. "You know?"

"I mean he might be tempted, but he hasn't been—as yet."

"You're sure?"

"I am."

In the end he believed that Peter was counselling me. After the interrogation, he brought me into a refectory for tea and a chocolate marshmallow. It was a bleak place, with a slop bucket beside the kitchen, which reminded me of school. No wonder Peter liked my flat, which was cosier, if damp. On the way home, I wondered how Father Power knew so much. The details of Peter waiting on the windowsill suggested that someone was watching us, observing from across the road perhaps? Maybe it wasn't Miss Walsh? Maybe another spy had written the letter? Declan? Was he mad at me for throwing him out? Or could it be Brigid, acting for my good? She hated any kind of deceit. Since loving Peter, I had entered the land of liars.

I rang Peter but he was out. So I left a message that everything had gone well and not to worry.

He didn't ring back.

Was I being shunned?

Twenty-two

DAYS PASSED AND no word from Peter: not even a thank you for lying on his behalf.

Why was he acting like this?

Then he rang, announcing flatly, "We have to end it, Louise."

It took me a minute to take it in. "I'm being shunned?"

"I told you, I could never shun you, but I'm under orders not to see you again."

"Who's ordering you?"

"My spiritual director."

"Isn't that the same as shunning me?"

"I've taken a vow of obedience."

I was sick of his vows and broke down crying.

"No one else will ever have me, I promise." His voice was upset. "Now please stop crying."

I couldn't.

"Please, Louise."

"I don't care who has you. They're welcome!"

I slammed down the phone.

I had to get on with my life.

I had sent Tim my article about ecumenism, but hadn't seen it in the paper. He had sent no more books for review and hadn't paid me for the last one. Maybe it had been reckless to quit my job, as I had the usual bills to pay. One afternoon a bus inspector demanded to see my ticket: I had paid sixpence for an eightpenny fare, trying to save tuppence. "Ticket, please!" he demanded, redfaced. I tried the usual stunt of looking everywhere for it. He started to take my name and address, so I had to produce it. He put me off at the next stop.

I had to get another job. I couldn't go back to the Claremont, so answered an ad for a helper at the United Arts Club and got taken on. The work was easy, assisting the chef with the evening dinners, then clearing up the kitchen. This time I had longer hours. It was often one or two in the morning before I was sent home in a taxi. But I didn't mind: it was liberating to get away from Miss Walsh. I was out of jail, although not free. I would never be free of Peter, or of the sorrow of losing our child.

I hadn't seen my mother for weeks. If I went home, it would be difficult to hide my unhappiness from her. But she was my mother and I couldn't stay away for ever, so I went home for Sunday lunch.

The meal was uneventful. She seemed calmer and said she was going regularly to her AA meetings. We were munching popcorn in front of the evening television, when I told her about Miss Walsh's treacherous letter.

There was a funny silence.

"It'll bring things to a head," she said, looking vague.

"Yes, it has, but wasn't it a ghastly thing to do?"

She went on munching.

"My friend might have been chucked out of the order."

She turned on me. "It's what he deserves!"

It was a change from the first time I had told her about Peter: no girly intrigue now. What had happened?

After a few seconds, I asked, "Are you drinking again?"

She was outraged. "No!"

"You're sure?"

"I promise."

She didn't have any other symptoms: no red face or slurred voice. I had to believe her. "What is it then?"

"That creep has used you."

"It was mutual."

"It's still wrong."

"He couldn't help falling in love."

"He could've ruined your life."

"Look, it just happened. You can't control these things."

My mother was now shaking with rage. "I hope he rots in hell for hurting you."

"You burn, if I remember rightly."

Anger was a bad sign. Then it dawned on me: *she* had written the letter! If I searched in the drawers, I'd find a box of lilac notepaper. "You *are* drinking again."

"I am not!"

"Yes, you are."

"How dare you say that!"

"Because you are. And you snitched on my friend. Admit it!"

"I will not!"

"I suppose he should be castrated."

She looked back at the TV. "Now you're exaggerating."

"Last time you were drinking, you rang up Nigel."

"It's not fair to remind me of things like that."

"No wonder he broke it off with me."

A long silence.

"You did it then?"

She was obstinate. "Did what?"

"Wrote to the master of studies."

"I don't know what you're talking about."

"How did you know who he was?"

After a few seconds, her lower lip trembled. "I knew his name was Peter; remember, you introduced us the day we met in town? Then I rang up Maynooth to find out his second name—I said I wanted to contact a priest who was doing a doctorate there. They told me where he lived. I couldn't stand by and see you hurt."

"You wrote on lilac notepaper?"

She was amazed. "How do you know that?"

"I saw it."

"Where?"

"I met the master of studies. I told him there was no truth in it."

I was angry. How could she? She was my own mother, yet she had betrayed me. She couldn't castrate Peter, so she had done so metaphorically. I could never tell her anything without it getting all over Dublin. And it brought back old hurts: memories of her drinking when I was a child.

"I'm sorry, darling," she said.

I couldn't speak.

"Will you ever forgive me?"

Once I had chased her down the road in my nightgown, but she had ignored me and gone into the pub anyway. My brother and I had stayed awake all night, waiting for her to come home. That was before the Canon had persuaded her to join AA. No wonder my brother had gone to London. He had left me to cope with everything.

My mother tried to make up.

"Do I have to get down on my knees?"

I didn't give in.

"I did it for you," she said.

I didn't answer.

"Please forgive me, darling."

If I overreacted, she would go back on the bottle. I had to get her back to AA. "He has to shun me now."

This incensed her again. *"What?"*

I shrugged. "It's canon law."

"What canon law?"

"Priests have to shun a woman if they've loved her."

"Well, the cheek! The bloody cheek!"

She went round the house muttering, "How dare they? How dare they?" in such a vehement way that I couldn't tell her anything about the miscarriage. God only knows what she'd do then. That evening I looked in the usual hiding places for whiskey bottles, but found none. She assured me she wasn't drinking, but the next morning I made her call in sick, then walked her to an AA meeting in Ranelagh and waited in a café while she attended. AA had worked in the past, and I prayed it would again.

At this time my interest in art began, the history of which was to be my life's work. I didn't know I would eventually go on to study for a PhD, but I needed something to distract me from Peter. So, inspired by Llewelyn, I got paper and pastels and drew an orange kite floating without an anchor over a bleak urban landscape. It was my inner state.

"What do you think?" I asked Llewelyn.

She scanned it briefly. "It's a good idea."

I pointed to the kite. "That's me."

"I know. The lines are . . . expressive."

"It's no good then?"

"It's a good *beginning.*" She picked an apple from the fruit bowl.

"Why don't you draw that? Hold it in your hand and draw it. Try to look at what you're drawing. Not the paper. Don't worry about making mistakes."

I did it and showed it to her.

"You need to slow down."

"It's terrible."

"It's not. That's how we learn, Louise. By falling on our asses."

Drawing became my new passion. I remembered what Llewelyn had said: I had fallen on my backside, OK. Would I learn anything from it?

A few days later, the landlady waved from her window as I opened the gate. What was wrong? Maybe Llewelyn had made too many demands—Americans were used to so much. Or maybe the curtains weren't drawn as instructed. No, one was distinctly fifteen inches over. How could I not have noticed? I walked up the path, pretending not to see her.

But she leant over the stone steps as I reached my basement door. She was wearing off-duty clothes: stretch pants and a long sweater over broad hips.

"Louise, dear."

"Yes, Miss Pym?"

"Could you spare a moment?"

"Eh—yes."

Oh God, I'd done something? Or had Llewelyn irritated her?

I mounted the steps to her hall door, smiling nervously. Maybe I wasn't done for? It might be a social visit. I was invited in to her cluttered sitting room. "A cup of tea?" she purred.

"Thank you."

While she was in the kitchen, her cat jumped on me.

"You don't mind Tammy?"

"No." I sneezed.

Finally Miss Pym noticed my discomfort and shooed the cat away, but didn't offer to put it outside. Tea was served in china cups, with sliced fruitcake on elegant matching side plates. I wondered what was up—she had never offered cake before, although she had probably given it to Nigel.

"I'm sure you miss Brigid," she began.

I nodded, my mouth full. Brigid was still the white-headed girl.

"How's the writing going?"

"Fine."

"You're making ends meet?"

Was she lowering the rent after all? I couldn't admit to being poor.

She put down her cup. "I have a proposal for you."

"Oh."

"I'm looking for someone to help my aunt with her memoirs."

"She's writing a book?"

"Yes, an account of her life. What do you think?"

I swallowed. "You want me to help her?"

"Yes, be a sort of ghost writer. Encourage her."

"Where do you want me to do it?"

"In her house. She's ninety-four and in a bit of a hurry."

"I understand."

So I was hired to go to the elder Miss Pym's home, interview her, then write her memories up as a book. It sounded easy and suited my qualifications. I had a job—at the princely sum of five pounds an hour. As much as I had earned in a day at the Arts Club.

Miss Pym senior was *the* Miss Pym. She lived in a nice house in Monkstown and was distinct from her niece by having no initial. This indicated her status.

"You two will get on, I know it," my landlady said, letting us in with her key. "Don't mind if she's grumpy. It's her age."

I followed her into a black and white tiled hall.

The house was dark and overheated. Miss Pym was in an armchair in the sitting room, wrapped in copious rugs. She had a hacking cough, and I had never seen anyone with such red-veined, leathery skin and watery eyes. I wondered if she had been jilted on her wedding eve, like Miss Havisham. There wasn't a cobweb in sight.

She offered me a gnarled hand. "Who is this?"

My landlady introduced me.

"Louise is going to help with your memoirs."

There was another fit of coughing. Then a wicked gleam appeared in the older woman's eye, as she gasped, "I told you, I don't want to write my memoirs."

"Now, now." Miss P. Pym ignored her and got us settled.

I was sitting in a chair opposite, and there was a tape recorder on the table between us. Then my landlady went shopping, promising to come back at the end of our session to make afternoon tea.

As soon as the door was shut, Miss Pym sat up straight. "Would you like a whiskey?"

I shook my head. "I don't like whiskey."

She waved in the direction of the kitchen. "Of course you do! Get a glass."

The glasses were in a pine dresser. When I came back, she took another glass and a whiskey bottle from under her rugs.

She poured me a drink, then topped up her own, holding a finger to her lips. "Now don't breathe a word!"

I promised not to, but had a *déjà vu* feeling. Why was it my lot to look after drinkers? I sipped the whiskey, which was horrible without ginger ale, making nervous enquiries about her childhood. Where she had been born and when?

"My niece gives me no peace," she complained in reply. "Don't pay any attention to her!"

"But I've been hired to help you, remember."

"Can't remember a thing!"

"Not even your childhood?"

"My niece needs a man. That's her problem."

I was afraid to mention Gordon, her niece's live-in boyfriend. Didn't she know about him?

"Jilted in her youth by a no-good," she went on. "She's had an unhappy life since."

Our landlady had always seemed happy.

"Do you have a young man, my dear?"

I shook my head.

"You're so young, and so handsome."

I felt myself blush. "Eh, thanks."

"You'll meet someone. Love is all there is in life. And you must have children."

The old lady looked so sad when she said this that I felt like crying too. A baby was a wonderful gift, and I had carelessly lost mine.

"You're drinking too quickly!" she shouted.

"Sorry."

I sipped the last of my whiskey.

She looked alarmed. "Now you want more?"

"Eh, no."

I was getting nowhere with the interview. But after a bit more prodding, the old lady gave in and told me she had been born in the last century and had had a fascinating life in India, a country which I had always wanted to visit. Then she started to tell me about her father and mother, but fell asleep in the middle.

I tried to wake her but couldn't.

She was in a drunken sleep.

Miss Pym the younger came back after an hour. She took in the situation immediately. "Oh, dear. There must be a bottle some place."

She searched among the rugs and found it. "She's not getting any more of that!"

I agreed that the old woman shouldn't be drinking, but, in a sense, what did it matter at her age?

My landlady turned to me. "I'll have to stay until she wakes up. Can you get the bus home?"

"Of course."

"I'm sorry, Louise—I don't think this is going to work."

She gave me five pounds from her handbag.

"It's OK," I said.

"Louise, we agreed on this."

She insisted, so I had to take it.

Soon after that, Miss Pym got her aunt into a nursing home, and I promised to visit her, although not for money. The old lady made me reflect on the human condition. Loneliness in this life must be the reason for inventing heaven in the next. I decided to apply for nursing in London and specialise in geriatric care. Life was difficult for everyone, but especially for the old. My troubles were nothing in the scheme of things.

Twenty-three

A MONTH PASSED with no word from Peter. His spiritual director had won. It was over.

Summer came with its long evenings, which compounded my unhappiness. It was six months since we had met. Now he had given me up without any thanks for saving him from being laicised. I wasn't even an affair, just a fling. I hated him, yet missed him equally. How had I been so foolish? D. H. Lawrence had been right: it was the way your sympathy flowed that really determined your life. That was in *Lady Chatterley's Lover.* Everyone had a secret river inside them, and Peter had discovered mine.

At the beginning of July, the Arts Club chef gave me a voucher for a free dinner for two in a new restaurant in the basement of Castletown House. It was a promotion, and you had to pay only for the wine. On impulse I phoned and invited Peter. It was foolish, I know. At first he pretended to be surprised to hear from me, then he said he was delighted and we could go, that no one would recognise him in County Kildare. He would borrow a visiting Canadian's Chevy and drive us down.

"Promise," I said.

"Oh, yeah," he drawled. "I want you to have some fun. I don't want to be a bad memory."

That sounded ominous.

It meant he was not coming back permanently, but he had said things like that before, so I had *some* hope that everything wasn't over. Maybe he would change his mind and we would end up together after all, on the missions in a remote place, where no one would know him and he could do good. I could be his helper.

The song "American Pie" was all the rage, so I started singing it to myself around the flat. I was going in a Chevy myself, and Peter was collecting me. It was almost a date. I rang and booked the table at Castletown. I even got a new pair of jeans and a shirt. On the night in question, I had a long bath and painted my toenails pink. I put on a face-mask and slices of cucumber on my eyes, like my mother used to do for her romantic assignations with my brother's teachers.

The hour came.

And passed.

I checked the street every few minutes.

No Peter.

Where was he? Had the car given him trouble? It was an old car, so that might be the case.

Then it dawned: I had been stood up.

For about an hour I sat looking at the damp walls, calling him all sorts of names in my head. Then I tore up my voucher in tears. I was finished with Peter: I wanted to cut off my breasts like Saint Agatha and serve them to him on a plate.

Yet it was a turning point for me. I rang Peter's monastery and left a message with the lay brother, saying that everything was over. The old man repeated it: "Everything is over?"

"Yes. Tell Father I have given up sin *for ever.*"

"You've given up sin for ever?"

"Yes. Father will understand."

"God bless you."

And he hung up.

My journalism had been shelved with all this passion. My non-career would never take off now. Peter had tried to help with my religious articles, but Tim still said they weren't critical enough. The church was in a rut, he claimed, and needed shaking up. I don't know what he thought I could do about that. It had been that way for the last 2,000 years. If John XXIII hadn't changed things, how could I?

Tim had rewritten my article on the ecumenical movement. He had added to it, criticising the lack of cooperation in Christian attitudes towards unification. It was embarrassing when I had said great things were being done by both sides. I took to wearing sunglasses around Sandymount, even on grey days, in case I bumped into Andrew, the director of the Ecumenical Centre. He was a polite man, but what would he think of me now? I must seem like a traitor to twist everything he had said. So I decided to tackle Tim about this head-on. Life was hard enough without dodging people.

As I went into the editorial office, Tim looked up from his typing. He was in shirt-sleeves and, as usual, smelled of sweat.

He smiled. "Ah hello, love."

I steeled myself. I never wanted to be called that again, not by any man. "Don't call me 'love'."

He looked surprised. "Well, sorry, love . . . eh, sorry. . ."

I held out a copy of the paper, showing my article.

"What is it?" he asked.

"I never wrote that."

He studied the paper. "No, but you should have."

"I don't think it's fair."

He shrugged. "Who said life had to be fair?"

"You can't change everything I write."

Tim went back to his work.

"I'm resigning then," I heard myself say over the rat-tat-tat.

He stopped typing, sighed and looked over the big table, littered with letters and invitations to this and that art gallery opening or theatrical first night. He picked out one, like from a lucky dip, squinted at it and handed it to me.

"Here, review this." It was an invitation to the first night of a play by Brian Friel at the Peacock Theatre: *Philadelphia, Here I Come!* "You can be a drama critic."

I was taken aback. "What?"

"We've no drama critic at the moment. Write me 300 words."

I stared at the invitation. How could I be a drama critic?

"I wouldn't know what to say."

Tim was unsympathetic to this view. "You've been to the theatre before?"

"Yes."

"Just be an ordinary punter. If you enjoy it, they will too. We only consider the cash customer here."

And he went back to typing.

I shouted over the noise. "Will you promise not to change my copy?"

He nodded at his typewriter.

I took the invitation and went back down the stairs, feeling somewhat better. I didn't know anything about drama, but that's journalism. You pretend to know. And, after all, I had a degree in English. I might as well use it.

The play was opening the next night. Brian Friel's title described the times: everyone was leaving Ireland. I arranged for an evening off work and got ready, having a long luxurious bath and washing my hair. I wore my new outfit, the one I had bought for the dinner at

Castletown House. But at the last minute I wasn't going to go. I was alone in my flat, like in the Liza Minnelli song from *Cabaret.* I still felt bruised about Peter standing me up and thought, to hell with Tim and his damn review. To hell with all men. I'd soon be studying nursing in London, where I would look after women only. I'd stay home that night and wallow in my misery. Then the words of the song came into my head. *"What good is sitting alone in your room . . . come to the cabaret . . ."*

I was still angry with my mother, but she loved Liza Minelli, and that song was stuck in my head because of her. *Life is a cabaret, old chum.* So if it hadn't been for my mother singing it, I might not have gone to the Peacock that night. Such is life.

Nigel was the first person I saw.

The little shit was in the lobby with Hilly. They were sipping wine at a table, waiting for the play to start.

I started to leave, then stopped myself. I couldn't run every time I saw Nigel. OK, so it had been a big disappointment being dumped by him, but he had had a right to give me up. He had wanted to move on. I had to grow up and accept that I wasn't God's gift to men: I attracted only unsuitable types who liked big breasts. Maybe the best thing would be to go into a convent like Héloïse—the Medical Missionaries of Mary might be a modern equivalent. That way I could combine nursing and religion. Everything would be taken care of. I wouldn't have to sweat it out in the Arts Club, washing dishes till the early hours to pay the rent. But it wasn't the Middle Ages, and I would never last in a convent.

I hid in the loo until the doors opened, then took my seat. Nigel was entering an aisle at the other side of the theatre, so I waved.

He looked surprised to see me, then whispered to Hilly, who was behind him.

We smiled at each other.

All through the first half, I tried to take notes for my review, but couldn't concentrate. I kept sneaking glances at Nigel, worrying about what I would do in the interval. Maybe I'd stay in my seat, but what if he came and talked to me? I would be trapped. Since Peter had shunned me, I felt naked. Everyone was staring at me.

I decided to hide in the loo again.

When the stage darkened for the interval, I went out to the lobby, making sure to get there ahead of Nigel and Hilly. Then I noticed a small man with Einstein hair, standing alone. He was the American professor from Bernardo's restaurant, when I had been footless. Jesus.

He was dressed in academic style, Levis and a tweed jacket, and was wearing his gold-rimmed glasses, while studying the programme. Just my luck—now I had two people to avoid.

With a thumping heart, I sneaked past him.

"Hi there!" he called after me.

I turned. "Hello."

"It's Louise, isn't it?"

"Yes."

"How have you been?"

It had to be a reference to my drunkenness. "Since I made a holy show of myself?"

He laughed. "I'd forgotten that."

"I was a disgrace."

"You got home all right? I called a cab, but the priest, what was his name?"

"Peter. Father Peter Fanning."

"He wanted to see you home."

I changed the subject. "You're Professor Scott?"

He looked grumpy.

"I was in your politics tutorial." I hesitated, laughing. "Sorry, I could never make it. I was always too busy writing history essays."

He continued to frown, taking off his glasses and putting them in his top pocket. "History essays?"

"I thought you didn't remember me in Bernardo's."

"I remembered you well."

God. "You did?"

"Eh—I'm not Scott. I'm Delaney, Dan Delaney."

"That's right," I said. "Sorry. Professor Scott was the other one."

I had said the wrong name. There were two Americans in college at the same time. I knew his name well, but the wrong one had come out. I always did this when stressed.

"You were both in UCD."

He nodded, staring.

I stood there awkwardly. What was I to say next? From the corner of my eye, I saw Nigel shouldering through the crowd towards us with Hilly in tow.

Dan Delaney broke the silence. "Well, what have you been doing since?"

"Since the Lincoln Inn? I wish you'd forget that."

"I meant since college?"

"This and that. It's hard to get a job. I'm thinking of nursing."

He frowned again. "Nursing?"

Nigel and Hilly had stopped to talk to someone else.

"I shouldn't have done arts."

He looked disappointed. "Why not?"

"No jobs, except for teachers."

"Well . . . you read a few books."

"I suppose so."

We chatted on. Then the bell went for the end of the interval. People started moving back to the theatre.

"Let's have a pint," he said. "I'll meet you here after the play."

"Here?"

He pointed to an emergency exit sign over my head. "Wait right here."

"OK."

"After the play. Don't forget."

"No," I laughed.

And we joined the rest of the audience returning to the theatre. I didn't see Nigel and Hilly anywhere. I only knew I had been invited for a drink by a man who wasn't afraid to be seen with me.

Twenty-four

THERE WAS A lovely intimacy in Dublin then. It wasn't like now, with stag weekends and puking teenagers; it was more bohemian. We went to a pub opposite the Peacock—The Plough, which was frequented by actors. There was smoke everywhere and someone was singing "The Wild Colonial Boy" from the corner. It was a huge relief to be there, having a drink openly. Not sipping the monastery's rusty Guinness at home. I'm not saying Peter could help it. He wasn't mean, but he had a vow of poverty, so we had never even gone to a pub together—we couldn't in case someone might recognise him. Except for a few times after work with Shane, then Father Pat in the Horse Show House, I hadn't been in a pub since the Lincoln. I didn't count the Claremont.

"What'll it be?" Dan was smiling now.

I asked for Guinness.

I watched him go up to the crowded bar, remembering college. Dan was a professor, yet had *us* for a tutorial. It was weird. Someone must've slipped up in the allocation department. Third years didn't normally get a renowned scholar. You had to be doing a thesis on the IRA or someone important in a political party. I remember Dan hadn't done anything on the course, but he talked about international topics and even about great books like *To the Finland Station.* It was mind-opening. A pity I had only gone a couple of times. I had never heard of Edmund Wilson and asked who he was. Dan had told me not to come back until I had read him.

That was just his way: rigorous. I never went back. Not because I was angry: I was too bogged down by life. I had so many books to read for history essays. Essays I could never finish. Now I regretted what I had missed. But would Dan remember my stupid question? I still hadn't read Edmund Wilson.

He didn't seem to. He came back with two overflowing pints, and a couple of packets of peanuts.

I stared at the Guinness. "Gosh."

"Oops!" He put a hand to his mouth, a gesture of his. "You wanted a glass?"

I clutched my pint. "No."

"I can change it."

"No, it's great."

"A pint will save me going back for more."

"Thanks."

I don't know why I was so touched by the pint. Maybe because Nigel had been so mean. He often pretended to forget his round if we were out with friends, and he always bought me a glass and said peanuts were fattening.

I nibbled mine.

Dan opened his packet. "Well, what have you been doing since college?"

I shrugged. "Different jobs."

"Are you married?"

I shook my head.

"You said something about nursing?"

"That's just an idea I got—for the future. I'm a journalist at the moment."

He looked interested.

"I'm reviewing the play. I'm eh, drama critic for *The Trumpet.*"

It was silly, but I couldn't admit to being a waitress. I wanted to sound important.

"The Trumpet?"

"It's a weekly." I changed the subject. "What did you think of the production?"

"Decent."

"You think it's a good play?"

"I do."

"He's a new playwright, isn't he?"

"He's had short stories in *The New Yorker.*"

I had to pick Dan's brains. How could I review Friel if I knew nothing about him? What would the cash customer think? That had been Tim's brief to me.

Dan told me he had met Friel in Derry when he was researching a book.

"I've interviewed him," he said. "It's in a book of interviews about the North."

I was impressed.

"My partner and I have published it. He helps me run the university press. He's my golf partner too," he explained. "My wife and I used to make a foursome with his wife."

I imagined them all playing in the sun. It was so different from my world.

So he was married. I had known, but didn't know how I knew. Maybe some people make an impression subconsciously—after all, the subconscious is the important part of us, of which we are unaware. And Dan had two children: a girl and a boy. I don't know how I knew that either, but I did. In college I had seen his big car in the Belfield car park and imagined their life in America. That was after I had left his tutorial, but he had stayed in my mind. Now we had met again. *"There are many events in the womb of time which will be delivered,"* Othello had said. Were we in the womb of time?

No, we couldn't be. Dan was married, and I didn't want another dead-end relationship. Besides, there were children involved. I had lost my own father and knew what that was like, so I could do nothing to hurt them.

We chatted on in the smokey pub. I can't remember about what. Then Mark McManus plonked down beside us, his hand held out. "Hello there, Dan."

Dan knew him well. "Mark, good to see you."

He was a famous Dublin theatre director. He looked like one, too, with long hair, a flamboyant cravat and open-toed sandals. That night he was a little under the weather—with drink. Still, after my own experience in the Lincoln Inn, I couldn't talk.

Dan introduced me. "This is Louise. She was my student a few years back."

Mark nodded approvingly, as Dan got more drinks. I thought Mark was staring at my bust, but that could have been my imagination. Anyway, he acted as if he liked me, and the word "student" sounded as if I had a brain.

Dan returned with the drinks, including another pint for me. I struggled through it as they chatted on about the different theatrical productions around town. What was on in the Abbey and what in the Gate, and the merits or otherwise of each production. The conversation got on to Behan. Mark had directed his plays, and they were talking about an upcoming production in New York. Again, it was all so far removed from my ordinary world.

At closing time, I stood up. "Thanks a lot."

Dan put a hand on my arm. "Wait."

"I'll miss the last bus."

"I'll get this man into a cab, then I'll see you home."

I was touched, but said it wasn't necessary.

He insisted.

"I'll be OK," I said.

"No, I'd prefer to see you home. You can't walk around Dublin in the dark."

I did all the time, but it was difficult to argue with Dan. He had authority from being a teacher, I suppose. Besides, Mark was far gone and singing an Irish ballad, so I had to help Dan guide him out of the pub.

We got him to a taxi rank. Mark was safely in the cab when he started kicking up that we were to go with him to Fairview where he lived and had a bottle of whiskey waiting.

Dan turned to me. "I can't leave him in this state. Would you mind helping me get him home?"

"No, I'd be glad to."

So we sat into the taxi, one each side of Mark, propping him up. Again, I had a *déjà vu* feeling about the last time I had been in a taxi and prayed that he wouldn't throw up on me. Had I been like that? It was enough to put me off drink for life.

Mark was singing a Behan song now: the one about the auld triangle on the banks of the Royal Canal.We arrived in Fairview and got him in the door of his poor-looking flat, up some stairs and into a narrow, unmade bed. Dan took off his sandals, and tucked him in. Then, just as we were leaving, one foot was raised.

"Socks, dear boy!" Mark said.

So Dan took off one sock.

Then Mark lifted the other socked foot.

"OK now?" Dan asked, taking that off too.

"Yes, old boy. That's a sweet girl you have."

I giggled, as Dan raised eyebrows at me.

After that Mark was happy to let us go, and we found ourselves waiting for a taxi in Fairview, because the buses had all gone. Naturally, none came. It was a time when there weren't many taxis, unlike now when they flit all over the city into the small hours.

"We'll have to walk," Dan said, after a while. "I'm sorry about this."

"I like walking."

It was true. So we strolled through the silent dreaming city in the warm sweet night. We crossed the Liffey and headed south to Sandymount. On the way, Dan told me all about his children who were in college. He asked again if I had never been married.

"Not yet."

"Never met anyone?"

"I'm a bit off it at the moment."

He was surprised. "Why so?"

"Oh, I have friends who aren't happy."

I hadn't. It came into my head because I couldn't explain about Peter.

"That's not to say marriage can't be happy," I added. "Good while it lasts."

Then Dan told me about his wife. They had separated a few years before, because of incompatibility. I didn't say: *you see, it doesn't work out.* He talked about some Arthur Miller play, where everyone was responsible for everyone else. It was a play about Miller's relationship with Marilyn Monroe. It turned out that Dan had lived near him in New York. His talk was intoxicating. It was so much more interesting than theology.

At the top of Serpentine Avenue, I told Dan not to come all the way down with me.

He walked on. "I insist."

"I can't ask you in."

"You can't?"

I pretended Llewelyn would object. "My flatmate will be asleep."

I wanted to say: *I don't really know you; I'm not that kind of girl.* Would he act like Peter? But he was a married man, and even if separated, the father of children. Maybe I was up the wrong tree?

He looked so disappointed, I knew I wasn't.

He walked me to the end of the road. "I hope I'll see you again."

"Sure," I said.

At my gate he wrote my phone number in a little brown address book.

"We'll have a bite some evening."

"Yes . . . thanks. That'd be great.'"

I made to shake hands, but he kissed me goodnight.

Twenty-five

DAN HAD DISAPPEARED back around the corner and up Serpentine Avenue when I noticed a figure lurking in the shadow of the house.

My heart missed a beat.

It was Peter.

"Hello," I said.

He didn't answer, but his anger was like electricity.

I found myself shaking. "I didn't see you."

He ran to the gate and stared up the road after Dan. "Who the hell was that?"

I was afraid to say anything.

Peter followed me to the basement door, breathing heavily as I unlocked it.

When we were inside, he turned on me. "I might have guessed."

I tried to explain. "He's the professor—"

"What professor?"

"You know him! Remember: we had liqueurs in the restaurant."

"What restaurant?"

"Bernardo's—where we met. Then we went to the Lincoln Inn."

He registered this. "It was Delaney?"

"Yes. He taught me in college."

"I didn't know you were so fast!"

"Fast?"

"Yes, wild."

"Wild?"

"You were *out* with another man!"

"We only walked home together."

He took this in, grinding his teeth. "Is that *all?*"

I'd never seen him like this.

"The last bus was gone and we couldn't get a taxi."

"He kissed you goodnight!"

"So what? It was friendship."

"It was more than that!"

"No, it wasn't. People kiss each other. In France they do it all the time."

Peter paced along the hall. I offered to make tea, but he wouldn't calm down. "I didn't like the look of him."

"Then why were you with him in Bernardo's?"

"That was accidental. We have a mutual friend."

"He's a lovely man."

Peter's eyes narrowed. "I can guess a man's character."

"What did you guess? That he's kind and wouldn't let me walk home alone?"

He looked as if he could hit me, but reined himself in, pacing the living room. There were tears in his eyes. "I've been worried sick about you!"

I was too tired to cry. "I'd never have guessed."

"You haven't guessed a lot of things, Louise."

What was he talking about?

Where had he been for the past weeks? I hadn't seen him since my interview with the master of studies when I had lied for him, perjured myself. Then he had stood me up for the dinner at Castletown House; had never even phoned to say he wasn't coming. He could have made up any excuse and I'd have believed him: mass, confessions, benediction, the stations of the cross, anything. OK, so I had come home late, but he shouldn't be checking up on me. I had never been home late before, until the job at the Arts Club. Not that it was his business. I was over twenty-one and he wasn't my parent.

"Look, we had to leave his friend home," I explained, "then walk all the way from Fairview. There were no taxis."

I babbled on about Mark being a famous director. And Dan had been my tutor in college, so had naturally asked me for a drink after the play I was reviewing. It was my new appointment at *The Trumpet.* What could be wrong with that?

"You were *out* with him? I can't take my eyes off you."

"We had a drink. After the play."

Peter was like a madman.

I reasoned with him. "You never turned up for our dinner in Castletown. I waited all evening."

"I can't go to a nightclub with you."

"It wasn't a nightclub, and you could've phoned."

"I'm an ordained priest."

"Priests can phone. And you never apologised."

"I apologise then."

"You're allowed to eat surely?"

'I can't go to a restaurant with a young woman. I've taken vows."

"I'm sick of your vows."

"Right, Louise. That's it!"

"Good!"

"We'll break it off here and now."

What was he talking about?

"I thought we *had!*" I yelled, not caring if Miss Pym heard.

We went on shouting at each other. I ended up crying and he got even more furious, then he said he was sorry again and consoled me, and this led to worse things. As always, I couldn't say no, but this time I didn't worry, since I had started the pill on Llewelyn's insistence.

Peter was so tired afterwards that he fell asleep. Afraid that he'd get into trouble at his monastery, I tried to wake him but couldn't, so he stayed the whole night for the first time. It was lovely to have him, like some sort of new commitment, but he left at six the next morning to say mass for the Poor Clares.

"I won't have time for confession," he groaned, pulling on his trousers.

"With Pat?"

He flattened his hair with my brush. "Yeah."

That's all I was: a sin. And Pat's woman friend was another.

Peter leant over the bed and kissed me goodbye. "I don't want you to see that man again."

I said not to worry.

"You have to be careful whom you associate with."

"You're paranoid."

"No, I'm not."

"He only walked me home."

He sighed heavily. "I don't know what's going to become of you."

And he went out into the Sandymount dawn, saying nothing about seeing or shunning me again. I fell back asleep, thinking it was lucky I was on the pill.

Twenty-six

I WAS UPSET by Peter's tantrum, but he didn't phone me the next day to say sorry. No, despite his appearance at the flat, our affair was over. There was no *Casablanca* ending. To pay more bills, I had to work two shifts in the Arts Club: afternoons as well as nights. And I couldn't concentrate on the theatre review either. Anyway, I knew nothing about plays. In Russia you have to study for years before you can become a critic. In Ireland any hack can do it. Tim would be mad, and it would be good riddance to my career, but Peter's jealousy had put everything out of my mind. I still hoped he'd phone me, but he didn't. He didn't come back to the flat either. I finally rang him, and he said he was still distressed by my fickleness, which was crazy, because I'd only had a drink with Dan. One lousy drink. And I'd probably never hear from him again. Men were like that—unromantic.

Around this time, Llewelyn got me a job for a week as an assistant at an art fair being held in the Royal Dublin Society. I had to look after the stand for the owner, who was called Richard. He sold her paintings along with his famous brother's. It was fun and better than the Arts Club, where I had been given back the evening shift only.

I sold a lot of paintings, and Llewelyn said maybe that was my gift, selling things. Every evening I went on to my other job. But on the last day, which was a Friday, I helped Richard and Llewelyn pack up the stand, and afterwards they invited me for a drink in The Horse Show House.

I was feeling happy, because Richard had paid me in cash. I had the envelope in my bag. He was older than Llewelyn, and I didn't at first realise there was something between them. We met another man called Tom Something in the pub, who owned a chain of shoe repair shops all over Dublin. He was small and dark and wore a suit. After a few drinks, Llewelyn said, "We're going for a meal; can you come, Louise?"

I didn't usually eat out, so I declined.

"Ah, come on, Louise," Tom put an arm around me.

I laughed and pushed him away. "No, I have to go to work."

"Call and say you're sick," Llewelyn insisted.

"I can't. . ."

"Please, Louise," she whispered. "I don't want to be alone with Richard."

That was how I ended up with Llewelyn and the two men.

First we went to a restaurant, then on to a nightclub in Leeson Street, The Firefly. I had never been in one before, and it surprised me that people were dancing, as well as drinking at little tables. Llewelyn seemed to be getting on well with the gallery owner, so I danced with Tom. I hadn't been to a dance since college and I enjoyed it. It was a change from sitting in the flat, waiting for Peter.

But the evening didn't end there.

When the nightclub closed in the small hours, Tom said, "We're all going to the Dublin mountains for coffee and some food."

"I'll head back to Sandymount," I said.

"Don't be a party poop," Tom said. "If you don't come, I can't go. I'm very fond of Richard."

I didn't quite get it that he couldn't go without me, but I didn't want to ruin the party, either. It had been a good night and Llewelyn looked happy. Besides, Tom had paid for my dinner.

"I don't want to waste money on a taxi home," I explained.

"I'll drive you home later."

So Tom chauffeured us all up to a big house in the Dublin mountains. I didn't know quite where it was in the dark, except that we passed Lamb Doyle's pub. On the way, Llewelyn and Richard were necking in the back of the car, and soon after we arrived in the house, which had huge rooms, they disappeared into an upstairs bedroom.

I was left staring at Tom.

"Are we having coffee?" I asked.

He laughed at me. "Don't drink coffee at night."

"Oh." It had been a trick.

Next thing his arms were around me.

I pulled back. "I'm engaged."

"I didn't get that impression in The Firefly."

"I'm sorry if you got the wrong impression. My fiancé's an academic."

"He's foolish to let you out of his sight."

"He has to study," I lied, wishing Peter were there.

We chatted on, as I got more and more nervous and Tom ogled me.

After a while, he yawned. "Can we go upstairs?"

"What?"

He grabbed me, touching my breast. "Come now, don't act the innocent."

I pushed him away. "Leave me alone!"

He leered at me. "You've been leading me on all night."

What was he talking about?

"I have not. You pushed me into coming. I want to go home now."

He laughed drunkenly.

"You promised me a lift."

"I'm too drunk."

That was true. He had suddenly got footless. I'd have to call a taxi.

As I looked for the phone, he made another grab at me, so I ran out to the hall.

I struggled with the front door, thinking he was coming after me, but I got it open and followed the spooky avenue to a narrow country road. It was inky black and I didn't know which way to go, but decided Dublin had to be downhill. I hoped to see a taxi, but two full ones passed. All the way I tried to sort things out in my mind. I had been an idiot, but had thought Tom was OK because of Llewelyn. But all men weren't the same. Dan Delaney had insisted on walking me home on my last night out. I had felt safe with him, but he would never contact me again. I walked until I saw the lights of the city and dawn breaking, only passing an empty taxi when almost home.

Llewelyn never mentioned the night, and neither did I. I felt too embarrassed.

About a week later, the phone was ringing as I got back from work. I unlocked the door and grabbed the receiver.

It was Dan.

"Hello." I was out of breath.

"I was about to hang up."

"Sorry, I just got in."

He laughed. "You're a hard woman to find in."

"I—I've been out a lot."

"Living it up?"

"No, working. I had a job in an art fair. Then my night job."

"How did the review go?"

"The review?" I didn't know what he meant.

"Weren't you reviewing Friel's play?"

"It went well, thanks to you," I lied. I hadn't written a word.

"Good. Listen, I'm tired of eating on my own. How about dinner?"

Dinner? A date! I couldn't believe it. A brilliant man wanted my company. Despite my busty boobs, he had valued my brain. We wouldn't have to avoid people or duck around corners. And I might have missed the call: on such threads hangs your fate. We made an arrangement to meet at Dobbins mews restaurant the next night. I had never been there and looked forward to it, arranging to get off work for the evening.

But what happened?

Peter arrived, just as I was drying my hair before heading for the restaurant. Brigid had taken her dryer, so I opened the door with a towel around my head.

"Hello." I stood there, an Arab in a headdress.

"Can I come in?"

"Aren't you shunning me?"

He frowned. "How could you think that? I've brought you a present."

He gave me a copy of the Jerusalem Bible.

It was heavy. "Eh, thanks."

"Well, can I come in?"

I swallowed. "You haven't called or phoned for ages."

"Let me come in."

"I'm drying my hair."

"Please, Louise. I want to talk to you."

It was hard to refuse Peter.

He came in and took over towelling my hair. "I'm sorry about last time."

This was a new tone. He must have been talking to Pat.

"I'm sorry for shouting at you."

"That's OK," I said into the towel, afraid to mention my dinner appointment.

When I did, he dropped the towel.

"I thought so!"

I stepped back from him. "I can't go on like this."

"Like what?"

"Waiting for you to phone. L-loving you."

"Remember, love is a big word."

"We're only going for a meal."

He picked up the towel and rubbed me hard. "You'll be married to him next."

"You're hurting me."

"Sorry, but I don't like him."

"Why not?"

"He's too old for you."

What was he talking about? Peter was well over thirty himself. Dan was thirty-seven, but age had always been the least relevant thing in the world to me. My father had been eleven years older than my mother, and they had been happy. They still would be, if he hadn't died. Anyway, Peter's predictions were stupid, and I told him so. He was jumping fences. Of all people, he ought to know men didn't rush into things.

My evening with Dan was one of those that stick in your mind. I'd like to say I made a brilliant impression on him, but I don't think so. I tried to sound intelligent, but he tended to smile at some of the things I said. I remember we got into an argument about whether film was a literary art. I kept saying it was—after all, there was a story. He said it was a visual art. I didn't agree. So in the end he said nothing. I remember we talked about the Algonquin and the round table where Dorothy Parker had sat with her writer friends. He said he'd often been there for a drink. Then we got on to teeth. He was shocked that I hadn't been to the dentist for two years. Americans were always flossing, I found out. It was an obsession.

Before we left, I put a teaspoon into my handbag to replenish the flat's supplies. Brigid and I had always done this when eating out. We were socialists and thought that wealth should be shared. It was one of the few illegal things she had done, apart from stealing loo paper from pubs.

"Is that necessary?" Dan said.

I was embarrassed. "I suppose not."

I put the spoon back. After all, spoons weren't that expensive.

To make conversation on the way home, I said I was going down to see Brigid that weekend. She had been inviting me to Kerry all summer, and if I didn't take her up on it soon, the school holidays would be over.

"That's a coincidence," Dan said. "I'm going to Kerry too."

"You are?"

"Yes, I have to check out something in Tralee."

"Brigid lives near Tralee."

"Perhaps we can go together?"

My alarms went off. It was out of the frying pan. . . . I had liked having dinner with Dan, but I'd had it with men, all men. And love was just a word. It meant nothing, and I never wanted to hear it again. I wanted to knit for the rest of my life, single stitch. Maybe live in some quiet retreat, far from the madding Peter. I was to him what drink was to an alcoholic. He had been obsessed. We both had been.

"What do you say we bus down together?" Dan said.

"Can we be travelling companions?"

He said nothing.

"Nothing else?" I insisted.

He smiled.

"Promise?" I said.

"Yes. I—I hope we might move on . . . to something more—eventually."

I couldn't believe it. I thought I'd made a desperate impression, about my teeth and all, yet he wanted to go to Kerry with me. But if he required anything more, I couldn't supply it.

"It's definitely over with your wife?"

"We've been legally separated for years. We live in different buildings."

I walked on. "I don't think there could be anything between us."

He sighed. "You have a boyfriend?"

I nodded. I couldn't tell anyone about Peter. It would be letting my country down or something. Dan would think I was an Irish cliché.

We met at Busáras the next morning and caught the Kerry bus. The journey was long, but the bus stopped halfway for the passengers to get coffee or tea and use the loo. I talked about American history all the way: the different Indian tribes and the settlement of Virginia. I knew all about the Elizabethan plantations. My arts degree was some good at last.

At Tralee, we got a taxi to Camp and found Brigid's house, down a little side road and almost on a beach. Love suited Brigid. She was tanned and windblown by swimming and the salty Kerry air. I had met her boyfriend, Sam, but didn't know him that well. Their romance had been a quick thing. And I'd once got into an argument with him about organic farming. It had been all my fault. I didn't know anything about the subject. I'd just had too much wine at dinner.

But he'd forgotten all that, and after dinner we played some sort of a game with the *I Ching.* I got a verse about a marrying maiden, and something about a man remaining at the well. That was Peter. He had to stay by the well, where people went for water, the vital element of life.

Brigid was impressed by Dan. It was a change for her to be impressed by anyone. But she raised her eyebrows in disbelief when I said we'd just met and it was a mere coincidence that we were going the same way. He had come down to check something out in Tralee library. She still didn't appear to believe me.

"It was fast work," she joked.

"No, we're only travelling companions," I insisted.

In the end she gave us separate beds. "I'm so relieved you didn't bring Peter. Is that over?"

I still couldn't admit that it was.

"Get rid of him, Louise."

I nodded weakly.

But life was more complex. There were more things in Heaven and earth than Brigid understood. You couldn't help loving someone. It came from somewhere deep in your psyche. You suffered a loss, like my father dying, and that created a need, a desperate need to be loved. That's how I explained myself to myself. I didn't know what had motivated Peter. I knew he didn't regard me as an equal. At best I could only be his typist, with maybe a bit of empirical intersubjectivity thrown in. From now on, I would stand up for myself.

I reminded Dan that he had to go to the library, so he disappeared to Tralee for an afternoon. Afterwards he wasn't very talkative about it. The next day we bussed from Camp village, through Annascaul to Dingle, where we booked into a B&B. We walked all one day, as far as Dunquin, and stopped in a pub for a pre-dinner drink. I had a pint of Guinness, but knocked it over when explaining something too enthusiastically.

Dan got me another.

I knocked that over, too.

The proprietor glared at me. I had broken two pint glasses. Dan offered to pay, but they wouldn't take the money, just refused to give me another drink.

"Do they think I'm drunk?" I went into stitches, which irritated the publican further.

We left before they threw us out, and looked for a restaurant to have dinner. It seemed unbelievable, but it was before the Celtic Tiger and there weren't any open, so we bought peanuts in another pub and set off on foot back to the B&B in the rain. We were getting on well, but on the way, I explained that we couldn't make love because of someone else.

"It's an Irish situation," I said.

Dan raised his eyebrows. "He's married?"

"No. A priest."

He was silent for a second. "Peter Fanning?"

I nodded.

He looked worried. "He didn't take advantage that day?"

"When I was drunk? God, no."

He gave me a long look. "Well, I hope he makes love to you."

It was the last reaction I'd expected. "You're not shocked?"

"You deserve someone to love you, Louise. I'd be shocked if he didn't."

It was the nicest thing I'd ever heard. We went to bed that night on nothing to eat but peanuts and Guinness. We talked for hours, each keeping to our own side of the bed. I told him about the night with Tom in the Dublin mountains, and how I had given the wrong impression. Dan got annoyed and said that because a man spends a pound on you doesn't mean that he owns you. He told me he'd been in love with a graduate student. Not one of his: someone he'd met at a conference. Now she'd got a job in another university far away, so they had split up.

"It's been lonely since," he said.

I took the hint. "Look, I'm sorry."

"You rested your head on my shoulder in the pub."

"Did I?"

"That'll keep me going."

When he said that, I was upset.

Dan put his arms around me. "What is it?"

"I'm not that kind of girl."

"What kind of girl?"

"Fast."

He hugged me, laughing.

"You don't think badly of me?"

He shook his head. "I'd never do that."

I fell asleep, feeling safe again.

We became lovers the next night in that dingy Dingle B&B. I had kissed Dan goodnight—I couldn't help it, then things went further. I suppose it was human nature: a man and a woman in a bed, with the wind howling outside, two orphans of the storm. I wish I could say it was great the first time, but nothing happened for me. I was too scared.

Dan was upset. "Don't I do anything for you?"

"I like you . . . but . . ."

Dan kissed me. "It's difficult for women."

"I'm sorry."

"You're emotionally drained."

It was true. I was afraid Peter would leap out of the wardrobe. It was crazy I know, but I imagined he had heard where we had gone and followed us. And he would pop up from behind a rock on our walks, or be sitting in a pub as we were drinking. I actually looked for him. Was I cracking up?

On the bus back to Dublin, Dan helped a woman with her cases. I watched him, thinking how kind he was, how happy I'd been with him for the last few days. You're meant to be happiest when you don't think about it, and I hadn't thought all the time I was in Kerry. When the bus got back to Dublin, it would be over. The phrase "a man of sorrows" came into my head. I knew Dan had been through hard times with his marriage, and a daughter had developed psychological problems. He had told me about it. How he felt so responsible and how you couldn't fight the culture. In his case the hippy-happy American culture.

We got back to Sandymount late.

As I opened the door, the flat was jammed with even more of Llewelyn's stuff. There was a new dining table. My bedroom was crammed, too, the bed moved to a corner to make room for the old table. The TV had already been banished there. The poor obsolete machine was like a family member during my life with Peter. It had been the only witness to our love, because I always turned it up to drown the noise.

I squeezed between the furniture and made my bed with clean sheets.

There was no sign of Llewelyn.

As soon as we were asleep, the phone rang.

I got the receiver in the hall.

It was Peter.

"Hello," I said, my stomach turning over.

"Where've you been?"

"In Kerry."

"Kerry?"

"I was visiting Brigid."

"I don't believe you."

"I was!"

"You went with that man!"

I managed to persuade him not to come over. This made him hang up on me. I didn't sleep all night, worrying about a knock on the window, but there wasn't one. At some hour in the night, Llewelyn came home. Next morning, by the time I got up to make coffee for Dan, she was in the living room, already working on a painting. She was superhuman.

Over breakfast, Dan admired her work.

"Wiry," she whispered, giving me the thumbs up after he'd gone.

Then she told me Peter had rung daily while I was away, asking when I was coming back. I felt a bit fickle changing Peter for Dan so quickly, but Llewelyn didn't think anything of it.

I had to go back to work, so arranged to meet Dan after my shift the next evening.

He arrived at the Arts Club before I was finished.

As he sat with a book, I brought him a pint. When the bar closed, I still had to clear the tables and wash up, so he helped me, causing the barman to ask who he was.

"A friend," I said.

Afterwards we went for a meal in a late night café in Rathmines. When I said we'd go Dutch, Dan wouldn't hear of it. I still couldn't believe he was paying. It was so different from Nigel.

As we walked back to Sandymount, he asked what I wanted out of life.

"I want to love someone I like."

"That's a good answer. Being in love isn't always loving. Why don't you come with me to New York?"

I walked on, alarmed. "That's a big decision."

"Think about it," he said. "Come for a vacation."

When we got to the flat, Peter was looking in the front room window. Oh God, he was spying on me again.

I pulled Dan behind a hedge. "Can we go to a B&B?"

Dan was firm. "No, we'll talk to him. It's too late for a B&B now."

There would be a shoot-out at the OK Corral.

"Please!"

"No, I can't stand all this *Sturm und Drang.*"

Dan used that German phrase a lot. I'd never heard it before, but it summed up Peter and me. Our affair had been like a grand opera.

"Do you want to come in for a cup of tea?" I asked Peter.

I was in an awful state, but Llewelyn heard us coming in and got up in her dressing gown, offering to make tea. She was a buffer state.

I set the tray in the kitchen, making faces towards the sitting room where the two men were eyeing each other like boxers before a fight.

Lellwelyn wrinkled her nose, whispering, "I like the *wiry* one better."

"You don't like tall men?"

She shook her head. "Wiry's better."

It was amazing how she simplified things.

There was no John Wayne row. Dan and Peter talked politely about the Irish weather, that cliché of conversation. Then Peter left and Dan and I went to bed. What else could we do? I didn't sleep but tossed and turned all night, worrying about what the future held. Maybe I should go to New York with Dan. After all, we'd met under an emergency exit sign. Maybe it was an omen.

Twenty-seven

DAN INVITED MY mother for afternoon tea in the Shelbourne, explaining that he wanted me to come to New York. It would be a vacation at least, he said, and promised to buy me a return ticket in case it didn't work. That pleased my mother, who pretended to be letting me go reluctantly. But afterwards she said that Dan was a dream—good husband material—and she would never speak to me again if I didn't go. It was my slice of life, and I couldn't leave it on the plate. She had already picked out a hat for the wedding, and she wanted it to take place in Dublin.

In July, Christopher Ewart-Biggs, the British ambassador, was murdered, and people worried again about violence coming to the south. Dan flew home: he had to prepare classes for the new semester. It was hard parting from him, but I was to follow as soon as I had packed up my flat. We had known each other for just under a month, yet it felt longer. Time is said to be an illusion. Well, it was true: some long periods in your life zoom past, while shorter ones stretch for ever. Our time had telescoped out, so that I seemed to have known Dan for years. I felt sure there was an explanation for this, maybe in higher physics. It was a mystery, the way all the heavy nuts and fruit rose to the top of the muesli jar.

I couldn't believe I would be starting a new life on a university campus in the most beautiful city in the world. It took a couple of weeks to get a US visitor's visa and move my things to my mother's garage. Llewelyn wanted to stay on at the flat, but Miss Pym wouldn't hear of it. Llewelyn was too difficult, she said. It was unfair: just because she had told the truth about the damp and wanted the place painted. Her requests had all been reasonable, but, as I said, it wasn't a good time to be a tenant in Ireland.

I was afraid Peter would reappear, or persuade me to change my mind about New York. I might weaken if I saw him again, so for safety I moved back to my mother's house and my old bedroom in Ranelagh.

I had tried to separate from my mother, but now I found myself staring at her, memorising the features of her face. I took mental photographs of the kitchen, the chipped blue willow-pattern plates we had always used, the small back garden and the tiny one at the front. My mother and I had long heart-to-hearts, like two teenagers.

It was a sleepover in a way, and the last of my youth. My mother and I had singing sessions, harmonising songs from *The Sound of Music* and *Cabaret.* She was particularly fond of *The King and I* and went round the house singing, *"On the clear understanding that this kind of thing can happen / Shall we dance? Shall we dance? Shall we dance?"*

"A pity you were never breastfed," she kept lamenting.

It was an obsession of hers, as if she'd failed me, or it had caused some sort of character flaw which accounted for all my mistakes and made me insecure, unlike William, who floated to the top of everything. I hadn't been strong enough to resist Peter. I could have told him to go the first day he called, but I had fallen for his good looks, for the words he had spoken. Now I had to take responsibility for my actions. It was nothing to do with the lack of my mother's milk.

"I've always been closer to you than your brother," she insisted.

I hugged her. "It shows you can't believe everything you read."

Then she got weepy. "I'll miss you. But at least I prised you away from El Creepo."

Sometimes doubts set in. I was still confused about Peter but tried not to think of him. From now on I'd matter to someone else.

"I'm not going for ever," I reasoned. "Dan's getting a sabbatical next year, so I'll be back. And it might be sooner."

"How come?"

"It mightn't work out."

She was horrified. "How could it not work out?"

That was my mother.

"Maybe it'll just be a vacation."

"It's love, Louise."

"Like you and Daddy?"

I knew she didn't like to talk about the past.

She thought for a minute. "It's when someone loves you for yourself."

"And not my yellow hair?"

She was puzzled. "You have red hair."

"It's Yeats: '. . . *love me for myself alone, and not my yellow hair.*'"

She wasn't listening. "Love is something expressed by deeds, not words."

With all her infatuations, I never knew she was such an expert, but didn't say so. I realised that I didn't know what the word meant. Peter had used it all the time, but he couldn't have meant it. Otherwise, he could never have shunned me, no matter what the order said.

"Well, in case things don't work out, I'll get you some cash," my mother said.

"I have a return ticket."

A week later she pushed five hundred dollars into my hands. She had re-mortgaged her house. "You'll need mad-money."

When in a good mood, she used Hollywood expressions.

Then I started having nightmares. I dreamt about my lost child, that he had been a boy and was born able to talk. He was somehow mixed up with Héloïse's baby. I had another dream in which my mother and I murdered Miss Walsh from the magazine. Then the body was discovered by Peter, who was going to inform on us to his superiors. I broke into the monastery and tried to get a sheaf of papers which would incriminate us. Next my mother and I made our escape to the airport, where we got a plane to the States. The plane went up through a hole in the roof to the sky, then swooped down to observe a ship on fire in the middle of the Atlantic. We finally got to New York where Dan was at Arrivals, but I didn't recognise him, so my mother and I went into the big city and got lost.

Peter found me by pestering Llewelyn. One day he rang me at my mother's.

"You can't go to the States," he said.

"Why not?"

"He's a married man. His wife might get angry with you."

"They've been separated for years."

"Louise, you have to consider others. It's time to grow up."

"You never considered me."

He gasped. "What did you say?"

"You never thought of me. My feelings."

"How could you say that?"

"Because it's true. You always talked about your vocation. What about mine?"

He laughed. "You haven't got a vocation."

"Everyone has."

"Well, I suppose you might be something practical; you're not reflective."

"Another Mary Magdalene?"

He cleared his throat. "I didn't say that."

"You thought it."

"What are you saying?"

"I *propositioned* you, remember?"

He slammed down the receiver.

One by one I said goodbye to my friends: Shane and Conchita; Felicity; I phoned Brigid and Sam in Kerry. Miss Pym invited me to a farewell tea. I visited her aunt, who had been moved to a nursing home in Bray, which served sherry at mid-morning, so that wasn't so bad. She gave me a going-away present of an Irish linen tablecloth, which I still have.

Canon FitzSimon also wanted to say goodbye. I was fond of him, but couldn't stand him knowing everything about me. My mother would have told him all about Dan too: how I was going to America with a new man. But the Canon had been kind, and I wanted to return his biography of Peter Abelard, so I went to his uncomfortably clean house beside the church.

The housekeeper showed me into the same reception room with the old mahogany bookcases. Waiting, I examined the titles again. There was so much to read. Would I ever get round to all the important books in the world?

"I'm getting married," I said, as soon as the Canon came in, his black robes swishing. It wasn't quite true, but I said it anyway.

He held up his hand. "Why rush into it?"

I was surprised.

He pointed me to a chair and sat down opposite. "You don't have to get married on my account."

I was taken aback. Then he laughed and so did I.

"I want you to be careful, Louise."

"What are you saying?"

"Men can be tricksters. The boy might have other women."

"He's not a boy and he doesn't."

The Canon sighed. "Your mother said there was an age difference."

"Does that matter?"

"You're at different stages of life."

"He wants me with him. That's good, isn't it?"

He looked sad. "You're just so young."

I didn't think so. You don't when you're twenty-five. Then everything is relative.

"I saw you eyeing the books," the Canon said. "Why don't you pick one?"

I chose *Talleyrand* by Duff Cooper. I knew he was a French statesman who had survived many regimes, and I liked the sound of his name.

"A survivor," the Canon said, "which we all have to be."

Again I thought what a pity he couldn't have married my mother. Surely the Church would be better off with a non-celibate clergy? It had to come some day, but it would be too late for the Canon and my mother. He would always remain a prisoner of his housekeeper. Peter had never wanted to marry, so he was OK. He didn't want the Church to change. That's why he had entered such a strict order. He approved of the Latin mass, the infallibility of the pope, patriarchy and the non-participation of women. He wanted some sort of Utopia on earth.

My ticket to the States was for 15 August. It was the feast of Our

Lady's Assumption into heaven, and I thought of myself as ascending to another life in a new country. What would America be like? In a way, I was going in search of myself. By coincidence, it was the anniversary of my father proposing to my mother, so the omens were good on two counts.

On the day of departure I awoke at dawn. My case was packed and waiting in the hall, and the taxi was ordered for six o'clock. I didn't want anyone seeing me to the airport. I looked around my bedroom for the last time. My childhood books were still there, along with my volumes of D.H. Lawrence and other books from college. And a teddy bear my father had bought me, so that I wouldn't be lonely when he once went away for a week. I thought about bringing it, but what would Dan think? No, I was an adult now. I had to grow up and leave the past behind.

My mother came into my room. "A cup of tea, darling."

I sipped it. "I'll miss you."

She sat on the bed. "No, you won't. You'll be living your own life."

I was worried. "Will you be OK?"

She put her hand on her heart. "I promise."

"You'll go to AA?"

"I told you I would."

"I have cold feet."

She got mad. "If you don't go, we're finished!"

I washed and dressed and waited in the hall with my suitcase. The taxi came, and my mother helped me drag it out to the sleeping street. As the driver heaved it into the boot, she hugged me goodbye.

"Remember to write."

I was unable to speak.

I got into the car, and as it pulled away she waved. I couldn't look back, fearing my resolve would weaken. The taxi turned the corner and drove through the quiet morning city. It had never been more beautiful to me: the quays where I had walked and bought second-hand books. The space in O'Connell Street where the Pillar had been before the IRA blew it up one March morning. Then Dorset Street, full of deserted houses like missing teeth, on past the street where I had worked with Shane and Miss Walsh. I had blamed her in the wrong about the letter because she had persecuted me, but the two things cancelled each other out; we were quits now. It couldn't have been easy living alone with her obsessions. Even though happy, I was sad. I was leaving my country and everything familiar. I had been to London only once, for a summer. Now I was crossing the Atlantic. Was I doing the right thing?

I checked in and went through security, nothing in those care-free days.

At the departure gate, a young nun wept as she said goodbye to her family.

I began to cry, too. I thought of all the millions who had left Ireland, in our time and in the past, back to Saint Brendan in the sixth century. That summer a sailing ship had followed his ocean route to the New World. The nun and I were members of a wandering race. Although I had rejected Catholicism for ever, without regret or recantation, we had something in common. She was leaving Ireland for the love of God, and I for a man I hardly knew. Dan had been kind to me, but was I that desperate? I didn't need to live through a man. I could go back now, claim my case and get a taxi home. Find another flat with Llewelyn, or maybe Miss Pym would let us stay on in Sandymount. But there was no going back in life.

Waiting to board, I choked up at the thought of Peter. It had been a bad end, more of a whimper than a bang. I'd probably never see him again. I would be a journalist in America. I'd prove him wrong about being unreflective and would get beyond the empirical. I wanted to say there were no hard feelings, not on my part anyway

I found a coin box, but it was broken.

From another, I dialled his monastery.

As it rang, I pictured that unfriendly place: the old lay brother hobbling through long, dark, cold corridors to the hall. After ages he answered, saying "hello" in a shaky voice.

I was nervous. "Can I speak to Father Fanning?"

"Father is not available."

Had he been told to say that? I'd never know.

I kept my voice steady. "I rang to say goodbye."

"Goodbye," he repeated.

"You'll give him my message?"

"Goodbye?"

"Yes."

"I will."

He hung up.

I joined the queue for New York.

Dan was waiting at JFK. His wild white hair stood out in the crowd, and I recognised him immediately, so my dream had been wrong. We stayed in the Algonquin on my first night in the city, because I had mentioned wanting to go there. It was an extravagance, but his way of welcoming me. There were liveried doormen who knew Dan by name. We had cocktails in a wood-lined lounge, and I ordered a "Parker" in honour of Dorothy Parker. Dan had bourbon and water and the next morning rang for breakfast in bed, which came with a Michaelmas daisy on the tray. That day we went to his apartment on the Upper West Side.

Epilogue

FOR A FEW years, I used to weep at operas, at Mimi singing *"O buon Marcello, aiuto!"* or any other great aria about lost love. Dan was puzzled, but never quizzed me. We recover from loss because memory fades. At some point the pain went out of losing Peter, and I realised he couldn't leave the priesthood for me. But I'd got my wish: I found ordinary happiness. I didn't fool myself that there weren't things to work out with Dan. Reality, a favourite word of Peter's, is often hard work. But Felicity was right: our relationship was blessed from the start.

Because I was pregnant, Dan and his wife rushed through their divorce. We got married, not before God but before the state of New York, a week before Owen was born, and my mother came for the wedding. I was huge, and she got a chance to wear her big hat. Afterwards we had lunch in the Plaza Hotel and a party that evening for our friends in our apartment. I know that the pain of Dan's loss will fade too. Although he isn't with me now, I have a place of my own and a community of friends and students. Do I end this story by saying that my life is happy? Or by lamenting that Peter never answered my email? I shouldn't have sent it, and he was right not to answer. But human nature doesn't change: like Héloïse, I had wanted "some word of comfort", but I didn't get it. I could tell myself my message never arrived, that it had fallen into cyberspace, or ended up in a lost letter department.

But I know it didn't.

Perhaps the recipient deleted it, because we can't go back in life.

Only sometimes we have to.

Christmas was difficult without Dan, but I got through it all right, going to a carol service in Christ Church, which was beside my hotel, and joining Felicity's family for dinner on the day. The next week, I found things to do. Late on New Year's Eve, my son phoned.

"Mom, did I wake you?"

I'd gone to bed early, but the New Year bells were ringing and had awoken me. "No, I was dozing."

I suspected he couldn't make it to Ireland after all. It was to do with his half-brother's marrow transplant.

His voice sounded anxious. "There's something . . ."

I sat up, unable to hear because of the bells. "It's Jim?"

"No."

"Is he going to be OK?" I held a finger in one ear.

"Yes, they found a donor."

"Oh, that's such a relief."

"They expect a full recovery."

"Weren't you two compatible?"

"No."

There was a silence, like he wanted to say something else. At my end the bells were still deafening.

"Can you hear the ringing?" I shouted into the phone.

"Yeah. Sorry to have missed New Year's."

There was a silence on the line. Something was wrong.

"What is it, Owen?"

More silence.

"You're not coming over?" I persisted.

"I am! That's not it."

"What then?"

"This might upset you."

I was getting worried. "Why don't you just tell me."

Was he trying to say that he was getting married in a hurry: he had got some girl into trouble? Or maybe he'd had an accident?

I got under the duvet to block out the bells. "Owen?"

"Yes, Mom."

"You know I have every confidence in you."

"I know."

"Look, what is it?"

"You don't know?"

"Of course I don't. What are you talking about?"

"Dad wasn't my father."

I jumped out of bed and walked to the window. What was he talking about?

"Mom?" The voice from my cell phone wasn't clear.

At last the bells stopped. "I'm still here, Owen."

My husband had loved all his children, but especially this son of middle age. Of course he had been his father.

"They tested me for Jimmy's bone marrow transplant. We're not related."

I couldn't take things in. "But Jimmy had a different mother. You would be different."

"We didn't have the same father. They know from the test."

I was in shock. Was it possible? My mind wouldn't work.

"Who is my father?"

"Owen . . ."

"Yes . . ."

There could only be one answer. I got my breath. "The line is bad. I'm still half-asleep. Can I ring you back in half an hour?"

It was a shock to me, but it must have been worse for Owen. Did he think I'd been deceiving him all these years? Well, I hadn't. My mind went back to the holiday Dan and I had taken together to see Brigid in Kerry, when he had said that being in love was not love. How he hadn't made love to me, although he had wanted to, because I was so emotionally messed up. We had made up for it the next night, of course, and that event had been burned into my memory: I had believed it to be the night of my son's conception. Could I have been already pregnant by Peter? I must have been. We had made love for the last time the night after my *first* meeting with Dan. We were meant to have given each other up, but Peter had been so incensed with jealousy that we had made love for one last time.

Although I had miscarried a first baby, I had never suspected another pregnancy with Peter. Or if I ever had, I had pushed it to the bottom of my subconscious. I had always believed that Owen was Dan's son; that when the pill hadn't worked because I wasn't taking it for long enough, that it had failed with *Dan.* Things started to add up: Owen was tall like Peter, while Dan had been short and muscular with that wild hair. Yet my brother and father had been tall, so I hadn't thought anything of it. Then other resemblances came rushing into my mind. Owen was charming and popular with women. In that he had taken after Peter. He was the same sort of driven person, but then Dan had been like that, too. I knew from my reading that Renoir had expressed ideas about heredity: he thought it was the parents who make the children, but *after* the birth. "A prince kidnapped by gypsies will steal chickens as other gypsies do," he used to say. So Dan had contributed more to Owen's personality than his real father.

I had met Peter only once more: the year after I left for the States. Dublin is a small, intimate city, and you tend to run into people. I was home for Christmas with Owen, then about seven months old. I had been breastfeeding, but on that day I had left him with his doting grandmother and walked into town for a coffee, intoxicated with my few hours of liberty. It was our first parting since Owen's birth.

I was so glad to be home. I remember Christmas carols in Grafton Street; a crib in a shop window; lights everywhere. In those far-off days, Bewley's had been waitress-service, so I sat at a table in the middle of the room, inhaling the wonderful scent of coffee and contemplating what cakes I would order. I had decided on a Mary cake when I noticed Peter at the next table. He was darker than I remembered and seemed even handsomer.

My heart had almost stopped, but he came over, saying, "I knew you'd come in here eventually."

I couldn't speak.

"I only had to wait long enough."

He joined me without being invited.

I was flustered. "Eh . . . it's good to see you again."

As his eyes rested on my front, I had a let-down of breast milk. Would the stain be noticed through my jumper? Luckily I was wearing two layers.

"You've put on a bit of weight," he said.

I reddened. "I suppose."

I was bloated from feeding the baby. Why was he still looking at me like that? The waitress came and took our orders, while Peter joked with her. He was still a lady-charmer.

As we chatted over coffee, a baby at the next table cried, cutting off our conversation. It's the saddest yet most hopeful sound in the world. I thought of Owen and all he would have to suffer in life. I wouldn't be able to protect him from the pain of love and regret.

I had another leak and covered the stain with my coat.

"You're cold?"

"No."

Peter looked irritably at the baby. "You can't escape from kids in this city."

Why hadn't I told him about my child then? I was a besotted mother; Owen was my pride and joy, yet I hadn't said a word about his existence. Had it been because of Peter's remark about the crying child? Or had it been because of his past relief at the loss of our own child?

We went on chatting. He said he had finished his degree and was waiting for the summons to return to his monastery in Canada. He expected to be given a teaching post in their novitiate. After more small talk, a young woman came over and he introduced us. I wondered if he was "saving" her, too, as he had always been "saving" me. She was confident and didn't look in need of salvation. As they chatted, I thought about what I had loved in Peter. Why had I allowed myself to be sucked in, never said no to his advances? Why had I been so needy? Looking back, it was obvious that my self-esteem was low, but no one had heard of the term then. It's a more modern malady.

When his friend left, Peter ordered more coffees. "Well, have you been doing any more journalism?"

I said I was studying for an art history degree.

"I've been living in New York."

"With the same gentleman?"

"Of course."

I hid my irritation. Why had he asked that? Who did he think I'd be living with? It was a typical Peter statement. He hadn't changed: women were Magdalenes or Madonnas, and I would always be in the first category. Despite being married and a new mother, I felt like some sort of stripper: his eyes were glued to my chest like the old days. It was the loss of his mother as a four-year-old, I had decided, which gave him this fixation. Surely all Canadians weren't like this?

"I suppose I should apologise," he said after a minute.

"For what?"

"I shouldn't have put you in that position. Had an affair with you."

I shrugged. "I wasn't a child."

"No, but you were vulnerable."

I laughed. "I was an idiot."

"I should have known how painful the miscarriage was for you."

I couldn't say anything.

More silence.

"Forgive me for being an asshole, Louise."

I smiled. "Now you're using bad language!"

"But do you . . . forgive me?"

"Of course."

I meant it. I had found love, but almost without looking and where I least expected to find it. I had swapped Heathcliff for Mr Darcy. If I hadn't been so badly burnt, I might not have recognised the real thing.

What did my son think of me now?

I had a shower, bracing myself, before ringing Owen back. I worried about how he would take the news. He and Dan had had a wonderful relationship. It would be a loss for him. Would he blame me? In America it would mean little to have had an affair with a priest, but Ireland was still full of Holy Joes. Many would condemn me, even though it was the twenty-first century.

"Dan was your father in every way," I said.

"I know, Mom," Owen was matter-of-fact, "but biologically, he couldn't have been."

"Biology is only one aspect of fatherhood. The father who raises you is more important."

We had reversed roles: I had a secret to tell him. "Your father is a monk," I said.

"What?"

"Peter Fanning, a Catholic priest."

He was silent for a few seconds. "You're sure?"

"Yes, Owen." What did he mean, was I *sure?*

There was another pause.

"It has to be him," I said. "There's no other possibility."

He still said nothing. Then, "How can I get in touch with him?"

"He's living in Alberta now—prior of a Bernardite monastery. You can Google him. When I knew him, he was doing a theology thesis in Maynooth College. It was before your father . . . I mean, our affair was just before I met Dan. But I never even suspected the truth until now."

"Did Dad?"

"I don't think so." If Dan had, he'd never said.

"You're sure?"

"I am. He loved you, Owen. He was so proud of you. You were just like him. . . . You both loved books."

"I thought I'd got all that stuff from him."

"But you did! He was overjoyed to have a literary child."

He didn't answer. God, was Owen mad with me?

"Are you OK?"

"Sure . . . I'm just trying to take all this in."

There was more silence.

I broke it. "Listen, I can't talk any more. I'm sending you an email. There'll be an attachment. It's a memoir I've been writing over the last few weeks, while waiting for you. I want you to read it without judging me."

My son still said nothing.

I was alarmed. "You won't judge me?"

"I'm not some green kid. Remember, I'm thirty years old."

"It tells the story of a few months in my life before you were conceived. The rest is up to you."

Another pause on the other end.

"Owen?"

"Yes."

"Are you OK?"

"Sure. Shaken and stirred, but OK."

I was relieved. "We didn't know, honestly. We would have told you."

"I know, Mom."

"Promise you don't think badly of me."

"I promise. Now get some sleep."

I saved my memoir onto a memory stick. Then I went downstairs to the hotel lobby where they had unlimited broadband for residents. There was no way back. I emailed my son the attachment, hesitating before hitting *send.*

I was awake all night, worrying about the reply.

It was there the next morning.

From *owen@delaney.org*

Re: memoir

I hesitated, then opened it.

> *I've been up all night, reading this. I couldn't put it down. I'm not sure what to think, or what to say. It's a shock, and it'll take some time to sink in. I've emailed Peter and asked for a meeting, saying you had given me his name. I'll be over in about a week. Love you, Owen.*

I had always felt that I had failed my mother in not becoming a romantic novelist, but now, thanks to Owen's mission of mercy, I have had the opportunity to tell my story. Throughout, I have tried to stay close to my younger self and have taken Muriel Spark's advice in *A Far Cry from Kensington* on how to write a novel: "You are writing a letter to a friend. This is a dear, close, friend, real—or better—invented in your mind like a fixation. Write privately, not publicly: without fear or timidity, right to the end of the letter, as if it were never going to be published."

Maybe this memoir would console my mother's ghost. She died several years ago. Llewelyn had been right in saying that there wasn't enough time in life, because she died young. Brigid is still farming in Kerry, a mother and a grandmother. Miss Walsh is no longer in the telephone book.

Over the years I have thought about my other, lost baby. Would it have been a boy or a girl? If it had been born, would my life have been different? Dan was such a tender man, he might have taken us both on. Then Owen wouldn't have existed. In the end, Peter had given me a real gift. It was better than the Jerusalem Bible, which I still have.

Last week I revisited Sandymount Green, where there were now several ritzy restaurants and an upgraded supermarket. I found our old flat on Serpentine Avenue. At first I stood at the gate, wondering if it was the same house. It was bigger than I remembered. Miss Pym would be long gone, and everything looked different. It had been refurbished with a modern extension at the side and was painted a dark olive green. A tree grew in the front garden, casting a shadow. I didn't recall any trees, only sunlight. Although we were all caught in youth's tangled briars, the grass had always been immaculately manicured. But where had Nigel parked his Mini? It must have been in front of the house; Miss Pym kept hers in the driveway. Nowadays there was a double yellow *No Parking* line on both sides of the street. What had become of Nigel? I assume he had risen to great heights at Trinity, but didn't know. I closed my eyes, and the smell of Brigid's greasy cabbage came back. In my head, I could hear young voices: Brigid arguing with Declan; Declan arguing with his French girlfriend. What had become of them? Or Shane and Conchita, who had lived over on the north-side? Had they ever visited me in Sandymount? Surely they had, but I couldn't remember them coming to dinner. Yet I remembered Shane sitting on the floor on a big green cushion, laughing his heart out about something. He had ridden off, gone like his cowboy hero, and would never come back. I had kept a painting of his for years, a white-washed stick figure on an old sack. Dan had always tried to throw it out. Had he and Conchita returned to Spain or Germany? Had life been good to them and their baby?

Owen phoned me again, saying that he had contacted Peter, who hadn't denied him. He was shocked by the idea of having a son and had refused a meeting for the moment, but would get back to him once he had absorbed the news. I felt most for my son, but it wasn't easy for anyone. Peter would also need time to adjust to a new situation. After all, he was the prior of a monastery. It's like in musical chairs: we had all lost our safe places and would have to find new ones. If you want a happy story, you must be careful where it ends—I read that somewhere.

But this story is no longer mine alone and, as all good stories do, ends at another beginning.

Endnote

HÉLOÏSE AND ABELARD, who are always referred to in that order, were an unusually modern couple. Their story has inspired poems, plays, novels, paintings, even a musical. Nine hundred years separate us, but only technology makes us different: people have the same emotions. Indeed, with regard to Catholic celibacy, things have hardly changed. If anything, it was more liberal in the twelfth century, since some priests were allowed to marry, but it was frowned on by the Church. Although my novel has a less brutal outcome, which says something for the passage of time, it has a similar cast of characters: a young woman, a monk, and a Canon.

Peter Abelard was born in 1079, the son of a minor Breton nobleman. His peripatetic youth led him to Paris, where he soon out-passed his teachers and started his own school, becoming the most important philosopher of his age. Students flocked to hear him from all over France. In 1115 he was nominated to the chair of philosophy in Nôtre Dame Cathedral and appointed a Canon, a step towards ordination.

Less is known about Héloïse's origins. She is thought to be the illegitimate daughter of a nun and was probably in her late teens when she met Abelard. At the time, she lived within the precincts of the cathedral and under the care of her uncle, Canon Fulbert. Abelard took lodgings in his house on the pretext of becoming her tutor. Soon everyone knew of their affair, apart from the unsuspecting Fulbert. On finding out, he was furious and separated the lovers, who continued to meet secretly. When Héloïse became pregnant and ran away with Abelard to his family home in Brittany, Fulbert became even angrier. Her son, Astralabius (or Astrolabe in English), was born there and named after a newly imported instrument for measuring the heavens. Abelard suggested a secret marriage so that his future as a great teacher, which at the time was impossible outside the Church, would not be jeopardised. Héloïse agreed to this, although she wanted him to remain free. When the marriage became public, owing to Fulbert's indiscretion, life became difficult for Héloïse, so she took refuge in the convent of Argenteuil, at her husband's bidding. Fulbert, wrongly believing his niece had been abandoned by her seducer, plotted revenge. He and others broke into Abelard's bedroom while he was asleep and castrated him. Although he survived, the priesthood was then canonically closed to Abelard. Neither could he function as a husband, so he entered a monastery and continued his philosophical work; Héloïse also remained in religious life, becoming a famous abbess.

Throughout his life, Abelard's originality of thought, which opposed the dogma of the day, made him many enemies. He spent miserable years in conflict with religious superiors, but always remained popular with his students and followers. When Héloïse's convent at Argenteuil was broken up ten years after their affair, he established her in another religious house, the Paraclete, near Nogent. As spiritual director, he visited her there, and they resumed their relationship on a professional basis, as founder and abbess. Abelard was musical and wrote many songs in praise of Héloïse. In e, he wrote his autobiography, *Historia Calamitatum,* as to a friend; Héloïse's letters in reply are considered the most ving of all time—she was never ashamed of her feelings. Abelard more difficult to understand: he claimed that the love affair was merely lust on his part. In old age, he turned to God. After he died in 1142, his remains were first buried in the priory of Saint Marcel, but later removed to the care of Héloïse at the Paraclete, where she was buried beside him in 1164. Their bones, which were moved yet again and survived the French Revolution, are now thought to lie in the cemetery of Père-Lachaise in eastern Paris, where lovers come from all over the world to seek help and consolation.